There was silence for such

there was a problem with Carl's antique cell phone. Finally,

Rose asked, "And so what happens if you get pregnant, and you're too young to actually have a baby?"

Defying all laws of inertia, the acceleration of Kennedy's heart rate crashed to a halt like a car plowing into a brick wall. "What do you mean?"

"Like, what if you're too young but you still get pregnant?"

"How young?" Kennedy spoke both words clearly and slowly, as if rushing might drive the timid voice away for good.

"Like thirteen."

Praise for *Unplanned*
by Alana Terry

"Deals with **one of the most difficult situations a pregnancy center could ever face**. The message is **powerful** and the story-telling **compelling**." ~ William Donovan, *Executive Director Anchorage Community Pregnancy Center*

"Alana Terry does an amazing job tackling a very **sensitive subject from the mother's perspective**." ~ Pamela McDonald, *Director Okanogan CareNet Pregnancy Center*

"**Thought-provoking** and intense ... Shows **different sides of the abortion argument**." ~ Sharee Stover, *Wordy Nerdy*

"Alana has a way of sharing the gospel **without being preachy**." ~ Phyllis Sather, *Purposeful Planning*

She wouldn't be victimized again. She had to get away. She wouldn't let him catch up to her. A footstep on the concrete. Not a fabrication. Not this time. It was real. Real as the scientific method. Real as her parents' love for her. Real as death. In the pitch darkness, she rushed ahead, running her fingers along the grimy wall so she would know which way to go as she sprinted down the walkway. What did contracting a few germs compare to getting murdered?

How close was he now? And why couldn't she have remembered her pepper spray? She strained her ears but only heard the slap of her boots on the walkway, the sound of her own panting, the pounding of her heart valves in her pericardial sac. She didn't want to stop, couldn't slow down, but she had to save her strength. She needed energy to fight back when he caught up. She couldn't hear him, but that didn't mean he wasn't coming.

Any second now.

Praise for *Paralyzed* by Alana Terry

"Alana Terry has **done the almost unthinkable**; she has written a story with **raw emotions of real people**, not the usual glossy Christian image." ~ Jasmine Augustine, Tell Tale Book Reviews

"Alana has a way of **using fiction to open difficult issues** and make you think." ~ Phyllis Sather, Author of *Purposeful Planning*

"Once again, Ms. Terry brings a **sensitive but important issue to the forefront** without giving an answer. She **leaves it up to the reader** to think about and decide." ~ Darla Meyer, Book Reviewer

Without warning, the officer punched Reuben in the gut. Reuben doubled over as the cop brought his knee up to his face. Reuben staggered.

"You dirty n — " Without warning, the cop whipped out his pistol and smashed its butt against Reuben's head. He crumpled to the ground, where the officer's boots were ready to meet him with several well-placed kicks.

Throwing all rational thoughts aside, Kennedy jumped on his back. Anything to get him to stop beating Reuben. The officer swore and swatted at her. Kennedy heard herself screaming but had no idea what she was saying. She couldn't see anything else, nor could she understand how it was that when her normal vision returned, she was lying on her back, but the officer and Reuben were nowhere to be seen.

Praise for *Policed* by Alana Terry

"*Policed* could be taken **from the headlines of today's news**." ~ Meagan Myhren-Bennett, *Blooming with Books*

"**A provocative story** with authentic characters." ~ Sheila McIntyre, *Book Reviewer*

"It is important for Christian novelists to address today's issues like police misconduct and racism. Too often writers tiptoe around **serious issues faced by society**." ~ Wesley Harris, *Law Enforcement Veteran*

"Focuses on a prevalent issue in today's society. Alana **pushes the boundaries more than any other Christian writer**." ~ Angie Stormer, *Readaholic Zone*

Wayne Abernathy, the Massachusetts state senator, was towering over a teenage boy who sat crumpled over the Lindgrens' dining room table.

"I don't care what you have to do to fix him," Wayne blasted at Carl.

Kennedy froze. Nobody heard her enter. Carl sat with his back to her, but she could still read the exhaustion in his posture.

Wayne brought his finger inches from the boy's nose. "Do whatever you have to do, Pastor. Either straighten him up, or so help me, he's got to find some other place to live."

Kennedy bit her lip, trying to decide if it would be more awkward to leave, make her presence known, or stay absolutely still.

Wayne's forehead beaded with sweat, and his voice quivered with conviction. "It's impossible for any son of mine to turn out gay."

Praise for *Straightened*

by Alana Terry

"Alana doesn't take a side, but she makes you really think. She **presents both sides of the argument in a very well-written way**." ~ Diane Higgins, *The Book Club Network*

"No matter what conviction you have on the subject, I'm fairly certain **you will find that this novel has a character who accurately represents that viewpoint**." ~ Justin, Avid Reader

"Alana Terry doesn't beat up her readers, but, rather she gets them to either examine their own beliefs or encourages them to **find out for themselves what they believe and what the Bible says**." ~ Jasmine Augustine, *Tell Tale Book Reviews*

She shook her head. "I don't know. I can't say. I just know that something is wrong here. It's not safe." She clenched his arm with white knuckles. "Please, I can't ... We have to ..." She bit her lip.

He frowned and let out a heavy sigh. "You're absolutely certain?"

She nodded faintly. "I think so."

"It's probably just nerves. It's been a hard week for all of us." There was a hopefulness in his voice but resignation in his eyes.

She sucked in her breath. "This is different. Please." She drew her son closer to her and lowered her voice. "For the children."

"All right." He unbuckled his seatbelt and signaled one of the flight attendants. "I'm so sorry to cause a problem," he told her when she arrived in the aisle, "but you need to get my family off this plane. Immediately."

Praise for *Turbulence* by Alana Terry

"This book is **hard to put down** and is a **suspenseful roller coaster of twists and turns**." ~ Karen Brooks, *The Book Club Network*

"I've enjoyed all of the Kennedy Stern novels so far, but **this one got to me in a more personal way** than the others have." ~ *Fiction Aficionado*

"I love that the author is **not afraid to deal with tough issues all believers deal with**." ~ Kit Hackett, *YWAM Missionary*

Note: The views of the characters in this novel do not necessarily reflect the views of the author, nor is their behavior necessarily being condoned.

Abridged

9781941735367
August, 2017

Cover design by Damonza.

www.alanaterry.com

Abridged

a novel by Alana Terry

"There is neither Jew nor Gentile, neither slave nor free, nor is there male and female, for you are all one in Christ Jesus."

Galatians 3:28

CHAPTER 1

"Hey, sorry I'm late." Kennedy gave her roommate a quick hug and glanced around the foyer of the church. "How's everything been going here?"

Willow ran her hand through her bleached hair. "Aside from the constant fighting, you mean?"

"Who's fighting? The kids from youth group?" Kennedy glanced around at a few of the teens who were helping set up for the upcoming Truth Warriors conference.

Willow fingered the neon-green tips of her hair. "Pastor Carl's bringing in nearly a thousand men to talk about the definition of *biblical masculinity*. You get one more guess to tell me who's making the loudest fuss about it around here."

"Nick?"

Willow smiled. "I swear if I weren't so in love with that man, I'd have duct taped his mouth shut by now."

"What's he saying? Or do I really want to know?"

"Oh, it's nothing that would surprise you. The typical. How chauvinistic it is to have a conference like this when it's the patriarchal society that's kept women oppressed as sex toys and domestic slaves for millennia." She rolled her eyes, accentuating the green eyeliner that perfectly matched her hair. "The funny thing is I agree with just about everything he's saying. At least on principle. But he's taking it all out on Carl, who might be a little old-school, but everybody knows he's the most kind-hearted, warm, fuzzy, teddy bear of a Christian you'll ever meet. There's not a mean-spirited bone in that man's body." She shook her head again. "Well, you know how worked up Nick gets."

"Yeah. Where is he now?" Kennedy asked.

Willow glanced down the hall. "Just keep your ears open. I'm sure you'll hear him soon enough."

As if on cue, Nick and Carl emerged from the sound room behind the sanctuary.

"And that's something else," Nick was saying. "You've got to open your eyes and see what this is doing to the community. You've got protestors threatening to march, maybe even block the entrances. You've got the police telling the church to tighten security and expecting St. Margaret's to foot the bill. You've even got the college kids around Cambridge so worked up they're writing their op-eds. I mean, even if you did feel strongly that this conference would be a benefit to the men who come, aren't you concerned about the way it's putting the church in such a negative light in the public eye?"

Kennedy and Willow exchanged smiles. Listening to Nick argue theology or politics with Pastor Carl was so common it was hardly more than background noise.

Kennedy glanced around, trying to figure out where she and her roommate might be needed. The girls were juniors now, back on campus after a wonderfully relaxing summer off. Kennedy's course load was the lightest it had ever been, only eighteen credits. In addition to her science classes, Kennedy was taking two English courses, including one in dystopian literature. Her schedule opened up time for her to get more involved in church, like helping with the after-school Good News Club and volunteering at St. Margaret's for special events like this conference.

Her roommate Willow was at the church now even more than Kennedy was, but of course her flourishing romance with the youth pastor had more to do with that than anything else. Still, it was amazing to watch how fast Willow's faith had matured. Kennedy didn't like to admit it, even to herself, but she often had to combat unexpected feelings of envy. Not just because Willow had found Nick. Anybody who spent more than two minutes with them knew they were a perfect match. In spite of the pain Kennedy had experienced in her own love life, it was difficult to begrudge her friend that happiness.

What made her jealous was how real Willow's relationship with Christ had become in just a few short months. Before her conversion, Willow's idea of fun on a Friday night involved multiple parties, multiple partners, and multiple illicit substances, but now she would invite Nick over to their dorm room where he'd sit in Willow's oversized beanbag chair strumming his guitar, and the two would sing worship songs before playing one of Willow's shooter games on her PC and ending the night in prayer.

Kennedy had never seen anyone change so dramatically. Willow was still just as outlandishly dressed, just as free-spirited with her hair and jewelry. She was just as committed to her veganism and yoga and classic rock music as she'd been before her salvation, but there was something else now, too. A depth, a maturity that made her seem at times like an entirely different person. Willow had developed a deep love of the Bible, especially the poetry books of the Old Testament. She spent as much time in Isaiah and Psalms as Kennedy had all semester with her reading list for her lit courses. Kennedy wouldn't be surprised if by Christmas break, she'd be the one asking Willow questions about prayer or worship or witnessing instead of the other way around.

"... not trying to pick a fight here." Carl's booming voice interrupted Kennedy's thoughts. She hadn't followed all of his argument with Nick, but apparently the two were far from any type of resolution. "But you have to realize that what I mean when I say *biblical masculinity* has nothing to do with what feminists talk about when they say *misogyny* or *patriarchy*. Is it true that some men and some entire church movements over the centuries have twisted certain passages of Scripture to keep women subdued? Unfortunately, yes. Does that mean that we throw out the doctrine of the inerrancy of Scripture and cut and paste the verses in the Bible that are acceptable to us in the twenty-first century? Absolutely not."

Nick followed Carl toward the hall, his blond dreadlocks streaking behind him like a bed of undulating snakes. "You're not listening to me. I'm not saying we throw out certain parts of Scripture. I'm just saying that there were undeniable biases in Paul's day that may have colored what he wrote."

"Oh, yeah?" Carl turned around. He'd lost about fifteen pounds since he was diagnosed with diabetes. His wife told Kennedy in confidence that he was "as prone to mood swings as a fourteen-year-old girl" now that he was forced to such a strict diet. When Kennedy noted the annoyance in

Carl's generally good-natured tone, she wondered if Sandy was right. "So tell me, Mr. Theologian. Tell me just how it is that you know with so much certainty which verses are God-breathed and inspired and which are simply guidelines meant to be followed in Paul's day but thrown out in ours. Because I'm sure itching to know how the Holy Spirit's revealed all this to you without breathing a hint of it to the rest of us who've spent our lives studying it." Carl brushed past Kennedy and Willow without looking at either of them.

Nick was nearly jogging to keep up his pace. "If the Bible's true for all people and at all times, then why don't you make every single woman who steps foot into St. Margaret's wear a shawl or handkerchief or other kind of head covering?"

"I don't have time for this." Carl waved his hand in the air. "I've got the press hounding me about this stupid protest, and I've got to get the church ready to receive a thousand men this weekend. To top it all off, my sugar levels are all over the map. I took my insulin but haven't had time to eat lunch yet thanks to all your incessant …" He turned around in the hallway. His shoulders drooped, and Kennedy noticed a hit of gray around his temples she'd never seen before. "Could we just finish this debate another time? I'm asking you as a friend in the Lord. Please?"

Nick sighed. "Ok. I'm sorry. I get so worked up over this kind of stuff."

Carl put his hand on Nick's shoulder. "I know, son. I know. And that's the way God wired you. I can appreciate that. It's just like Ecclesiastes says though, there's a time and place for everything. Understand?"

Nick nodded.

Carl extended his hand. "Brothers?"

"Yeah. Brothers."

Carl excused himself, and Nick turned around and offered Willow a sheepish smile. He walked up to her and pecked her on the cheek. "How's my girl?"

"First of all, I'm nobody's girl." Willow grinned and swept one of his unruly dreadlocks out of his face. "Other than that, I'm fine. But are you sure you want to get Carl so worked up? I mean, he's on blood-sugar medication and heaven knows what else. You need to be careful, or you'll give the poor man a heart attack."

Nick didn't quite meet Willow's gaze. "Who, Carl? He's strong. He can take it. He's been handling me for years."

Willow kissed him on the cheek. "Just remember your manners, all right?"

He took her hand and squeezed it. "Will do." He nodded to Kennedy. "How's it going?"

"Pretty good." Kennedy didn't know why she felt uneasy. Carl and Nick fought all the time. It was one of the great mysteries of St. Margaret's Church how the two of them got along well enough to work together in the first place, although according to Sandy there was a long, complicated back story that allowed each of them to overlook so many of their inherent differences.

"You ready to get to work?" Nick asked.

Kennedy nodded. "That's what we're here for. How's it going so far?"

Nick looked around. "Great. At the current rate, we should be ready for the conference in about six months." He let out a laugh that nobody else shared then cleared his throat. "Ok, how do you both feel about stacking chairs in the sanctuary?"

Kennedy glanced down at her tennis shoes, which were in perfect working condition. "Sounds good."

"All right." Nick gave Willow one more light kiss. "I'm gonna go talk to Carl."

Willow wrapped her arms around him to lock him in place. "Give him some time. He's under a lot of stress, and you can't blame him for that. The media's treating this whole conference like it's some convention for wife beaters or Klan members. And on top of that he's got you to deal with. Let him cool down a little."

Nick nuzzled his face into her hair. "I'm not going over there to argue. I'm going to apologize." He laughed at Willow's incredulous expression. "What? You don't think I'm capable of saying *I'm sorry*?"

"Oh, sure you are." She laughed. "I can hear it right now. *Carl, I'm sorry that I chose such a bad time to bring up the fact that this conference you've spent the past half year planning is actually nothing more than a bunch of misogynists getting together to come up with new ways to keep women subjugated like they've been throughout human history.*"

Nick let out a chuckle that didn't sound as convincing as he probably hoped it would be. "No, it'll be a real apology. Promise."

Willow rolled her eyes. "If you say so. Don't let me stand in your way."

After a few more kisses and endearing exchanges, Nick made his way down the hall toward Carl's office.

"Come on." Willow took Kennedy by the elbow and adjusted her long-feathered earrings. "Those chairs aren't going to stack themselves."

CHAPTER 2

"Is this about as high as you think we should go?" Cocking her head to the side, Willow stared at a column of chairs the girls had pushed against the wall. "Dude, I really shouldn't have worn these shoes."

Kennedy glanced down at Willow's open-toed platform sandals. "Think you'd be more comfortable if you just took them off?"

Willow shrugged. "It's all right. My own fault, really, my punishment for being vain." She smiled to show Kennedy she wasn't serious. "Ok, should we start the ones on the other side now?"

Kennedy didn't want to admit how tired she was. Apparently, reading books all day and working in science labs didn't require that much muscle. She wasn't built for pushing, stacking, and moving hundreds of chairs in a single afternoon. Although she appreciated Nick's commitment to gender equality, she wouldn't have complained if he handed this job over to a bunch of the teen boys from his youth group.

She sat in one of the chairs. "I just need a short break."

Willow plopped down beside her even though Kennedy was sure her roommate could keep up this kind of manual work for hours. Who would have thought yoga built up such impressive endurance? Of course, Willow labored all summer around her parents' farm in rural Alaska. Kennedy had spent the first several weeks of her vacation at the Winters', learning how to milk goats, catch unruly piglets, and muck out chicken stalls. It was no wonder Willow was so fit and toned.

Kennedy leaned back in the chair she was sitting in, panting slightly. In a way, it actually felt good to be breathless for a reason other than an imminent panic attack. After her month in Alaska with Willow, Kennedy had flown back to the East Coast where her parents rented a little cottage so they could spend the rest of the summer in Cape Cod. Her mom and dad needed a break from their missionary work and overseas printing business, and Kennedy was thrilled for some time off her grueling academic schedule. While at the Cape, her parents found a psychiatrist who decided to write Kennedy a prescription for her anxiety. The medicine could take quite a while to fully incorporate into her system, and they'd already had to adjust the dose a couple times, but so far Kennedy was hopeful the worst of her PTSD was behind her. What really convinced her parents to take her to the psychiatrist wasn't the panic though, but the depression she'd fallen into after what happened last spring. Kennedy was glad that the medicine allowed her to get out of bed each day. She was thankful the drugs helped her progress past the stage where walking from one room to another was enough to sap all the energy out of her system, but in a way, she wondered if she shouldn't rely on her pills so much. Ironically, Dominic was the only Christian she'd been close to who was against prescription meds for things like anxiety or depression, and it was losing him that dragged her to the point where she had to accept a little psychiatric help.

"Should we go find Nick?" Willow asked.

"Hmm?" Kennedy had been busy brooding and wasn't paying attention.

"I said should we find Nick? See if he has another job for us to tackle for a little while? My feet are killing me. I could use a change of pace, and it looks like you could, too."

Kennedy grinned. "How about I give you my shoes and cheer for you while you finish?"

Willow stood. "Come on. Let's go see what he's up to. If I find out he's goaded Carl into another one of his arguments …"

"I think Carl's just as guilty as Nick when it comes to that."

Willow shrugged. "I guess you're probably right. Well, let's make sure neither one is misbehaving, then."

They walked down the hallway, and Kennedy noticed Willow limping slightly in her platform sandals. They slowed their pace when they got closer to Carl's office and heard Nick's angry voice on the other side of the closed door.

"… bunch of wife-abusing, fundamentalist pigs."

Kennedy and Willow glanced at each other. Unfortunately, Kennedy couldn't say she was surprised to find the two had resumed their fight.

"You know that's not fair, and you know that's not what we stand for." Carl's voice was steady but just as elevated as Nick's.

"Of course you won't admit that's what you stand for. But what are you doing to change the status quo? What are you doing to elevate the women in our church to their proper place? Do you know how long it's been since you've called on a woman to offer the opening prayer? The opening prayer! It's not like you'd be asking her to preach from the Bible, heaven forbid. Or are you going to tell me that women are barred from praying in church?"

"I never said that."

"No, but you spend so much time focusing on the verses that say women should be silent in church, that they shouldn't teach or hold positions of authority. Have you forgotten all the women Paul addresses at the end of his epistles, women like Priscilla or Lydia who were just as involved in ministry as the most active of men in their day? Or maybe you've forgotten his instructions that when a woman prophesies in church, she should do it with her head covered. You don't seem to care what women do with their hair these days. You're fine saying that was just a cultural suggestion for the people of ancient Corinth, but Paul obviously didn't have a problem with a prophetess addressing the congregation. So she can prophesy, speak the very words of God, but she can't be one of the ushers who stands in the aisle to collect the offering basket?"

Kennedy shifted her weight uneasily. "Maybe we should come back later," she mumbled.

Willow sighed, her disappointment etched clearly in her expression. "I hate when he gets so worked up. I mean, I see what he's doing, but this isn't the way to change anybody's mind." She shook her head.

Kennedy took Willow gently by the arm. "Come on. We've had our break. Let's see how many more chairs we can stack up."

Willow glanced once more at the door to Carl's office. Carl's reply was too low to hear, but Nick's response was even more vehement than before. "You keep Willow out of this."

Both girls stopped and turned around.

Nick's voice was so loud Kennedy was surprised the walls of the hallway weren't vibrating. "This has nothing to do with who I do or don't plan to marry."

"Marry?" Kennedy stared at her roommate.

Willow fingered her feathered earring. "That's not supposed to be common knowledge yet."

Kennedy couldn't believe what she was hearing.

"I told you to keep her out of this," Nick yelled. "This isn't about her."

Kennedy tugged on Willow's arm. "We should go."

Willow nodded but didn't move. Something crashed in Carl's office. Kennedy flinched.

"Get out." Carl's voice was low and steady the first time but escalated when he had to repeat himself. "I told you to get out."

Kennedy would have preferred to run down the hall, but Willow's silly sandals only allowed the two of them to get a couple feet away from the door before Nick barged out, slamming it shut behind him. "That man!" He started when he saw Kennedy and Willow. "Oh, I mean, umm … what are you guys doing here?"

"Wanted to see where you were." Willow seemed perfectly content to let Nick hear the annoyance in her voice. "And how's good old Pastor Carl doing?" she asked with sarcastic sweetness. "Did he appreciate your little apology?"

Nick shook his head. "Don't ask."

Willow placed her arm on his shoulder. "Come on. You know I'm just giving you a hard time. You wanna talk about it? Would that help make things better?"

He shook his head. "You won't believe that kind of bull-headed arrogance. Makes me so mad."

"Come on." Willow laid her head against his shoulder. "Let's go to the library or something, ok? Kennedy, think you could give us a few minutes?"

"Of course."

"Come on." Willow spoke soothingly. Like a mother comforting a petulant toddler. "Let's find someplace quiet, and we can talk about whatever you want, all right?"

Kennedy watched them turn down the hall, unable to explain the deep level of sadness, an ever-tumultuous sea of emptiness that crashed around her.

CHAPTER 3

When Kennedy reached the sanctuary, she was more than grateful to find some of the youth group students stacking up the last of the chairs. She walked back to the main entrance looking for someone who might have work for her.

"You here to set up?"

She turned around to see Dawn, Carl's middle-aged secretary.

Kennedy gave a brief smile, which wasn't returned. "Yeah, I was just wondering if there were any jobs for me to do."

Dawn rolled her eyes. "Plenty of jobs, I'm sure. It's figuring out which ones need to get done first that's the big problem."

Kennedy didn't know what to say. She didn't know Dawn all that well, and even though their past exchanges had been cordial, Kennedy never felt perfectly comfortable around her.

"I'm sure Nick will have an idea of how you can help. I've got to meet my husband for lunch." With that, Dawn swept past.

Kennedy looked around at all the half-opened boxes in the foyer. It was strange. She'd never thought before of how much work went into planning one of these big conferences. She remembered her dad attending something like this back when they still lived in the States. It was so long ago she could hardly remember any details. What stood out most in her mind was how after one men's event, her dad had come home, knelt in front of her, and asked her to forgive him for not being the kind of father he should have been. She didn't know if things changed after his emotional speech. She just remembered the way his words had terrified her. Back when the world was black and white, when there were good guys and bad guys and it was so easy to tell one from the other, she thought that her father's apology put him on the same level as the villains in her Saturday morning cartoons.

What surprised her now was how many people were scandalized at the thought of the Truth Warriors conference. Back as a kid in New York, she recalled several events like this one. Nobody thought much of it, but she remembered listening to announcements year after year, hearing testimonies of men when they returned home from these sorts of conferences and announced before their God, their family, and their church how encouraged they'd been and inspired to embrace their calling as humble, loving, strong leaders. What was controversial about that? When protestors threatened to march in front of the church if Carl didn't cancel the gathering, she initially thought their complaint was that it was a men's-only event, which seemed ironic since who would bother complaining or boycotting a church that put on a weekend women's retreat?

As the controversy escalated, she skimmed enough news headlines to understand there was more to these protestors' grievances than simple gender-based exclusion. They complained against anything patriarchal, especially traditional religious mores. The feminists were afraid that an all-male conference whose stated goal was to encourage men to embrace their God-given roles as the heads of their families would send waves of oppression cascading throughout the church.

At first, Kennedy had stayed on the sidelines of the debate. She knew enough to understand that women's roles in today's society were freer than they'd ever been, at least in the United States. Leaders in the women's movement in the past had suffered and worked hard, and as a result, Kennedy could get a driver's license, register to vote, attend medical school, and become a top-ranking, respected doctor in whatever field she decided to enter. Of course, there were still many parts of the world where girls weren't given these sorts of opportunities, and one of her hopes for her future was to use her position as a doctor to travel to other countries offering health care and educational opportunities to girls and women trapped in these backwards settings. But that was as far as she'd ever considered feminism or the women's rights movement. She wasn't ready to go out and burn her bra or make the world bow down to her because she had two X chromosomes, but she certainly didn't want to take her educational and vocational opportunities for granted either.

As far as a woman's role went, Kennedy had grown up in a traditional family. Her mom kept house, and her dad worked long hours. But Kennedy knew plenty of other godly, Christian couples where both spouses held gainful employment. She figured those sorts of decisions could vary from one family to the next. She certainly didn't want a pastor to tell her the only job she could do was stay home and have babies, but she also didn't feel like she needed a whole army of angry feminists marching or making women feel bad if they chose to focus on their children instead of their careers.

Which is exactly what they'd done to Sandy. Sandy, the most maternal, godly woman Kennedy had ever met. But because she wasn't using her college degree to earn money as a "productive" member of society, the Harvard editorial team had ridiculed her in last week's edition of the student paper. All because she was a stay-at-home mom married to a pastor who dared to host a Truth Warriors conference at his church. Did these students know how many foster children Sandy had saved from a life on the streets? Did they know how much time she devoted every week volunteering for different causes? Just how did these editors define what *productive* meant anyway? Kennedy had never known a harder working woman.

"That you, Kennedy?"

She turned around to see Carl and Sandy's son Woong wandering the St. Margaret halls. "Hey, bud. What are you doing?"

"I'm supposed to be helping set up for the conference thing, except most of the time the jobs are too big for me, so I'm mostly just walking around."

"I'm a little lost myself." Kennedy was amazed at how fast Woong had grown. He'd gained half a foot over the summer alone. This fall, the Lindgrens had decided to pull him out of Medford Academy and teach him at home. Sandy had a feeling he was older than they initially guessed based on his scant orphanage records. She figured that homeschooling would allow him to excel past his assumed level in some areas (like science, where his curiosity had proved to be his most valuable asset) and would allow her to give him individualized attention to catch up on his weaker subjects like math and reading without the stigma of performing beneath a certain grade level.

Woong let out a loud sigh. "Hey, you know if they got any snacks? I'm hungry."

Kennedy shook her head. "Sorry, bud. I haven't seen anything around here. Maybe you should ask your mom."

He frowned. "No, she went into the prayer room with one of the teens. I don't know which one, but she was crying, so that means they'll be in there for hours. But it's ok. Hey, you know what? My dad was in a really big fight. I could hear him yelling all the way from the other side of the church. Did you hear it, too?"

Kennedy smiled at the slight exaggeration. "Yeah, sometimes even grownups get into arguments."

He shook his head. "No, this wasn't just the kind of thing where they talk angry and then lie and tell you they weren't really fighting. I'm talking about a real, actual fight. Like in those Jackie Chan movies. You ever seen him?"

"What do you mean?"

"I mean the old Chinese man who does kung fu and beats up all the bad guys ten at a time and then puts on his glasses and smiles real big."

"I know who Jackie Chan is. I meant why do you think that's the kind of argument your dad was in?"

Woong stretched himself to his full height. "I heard it. You know. Fighting sounds. Like *oof* and *pow* and *ahh* and things like that. And at one point a whole bunch of books fell over. Or something else real heavy and loud, but it sure sounded like books to me even though I couldn't see it on account of the door being shut."

Kennedy still hadn't decided if Woong's imagination had taken over or if there was really any reason to be concerned. She knew that Nick could be quick tempered when he was debating issues of social justice. She also suspected Sandy was at least partially right when she said Carl had been grumpier than normal although Kennedy wasn't certain if that could be blamed on the diet or not. But still, Nick was the most committed pacifist she'd ever met, and even though Carl could be intimidating, she doubted he had actually hurt a living being since his days as a professional NFL linebacker decades earlier. She figured Woong must be exaggerating, and who could blame him — stuck here wandering the church with nothing to do but stay out of people's way?

She felt in her pockets. She still had a few coins from when she'd bought her ticket for the T ride to St. Margaret's. "Hey, want to come with me to the vending machines? I'll find you a snack, and then after we've had something to eat we can look around for a job for the two of us to work on. How's that sound?"

Woong eyed the coins in Kennedy's hand. "How much money you got there, anyway?"

"Enough for you to get one thing."

He let out a melodramatic sigh. "I guess I'll have to be content with that."

When they turned down the hall toward the vending machines, Nick was running toward them and almost knocked Woong over. "Have you seen Sandy?" he blurted without a hint of apology.

Something was wrong. Something wasn't right.

"Sandy," he repeated. "I need to know where she is."

Kennedy's synapses hadn't connected her tongue to her brain quite yet. She stared at Nick's hands.

His wet, blood-stained hands.

"Holy macaroni!" Woong exclaimed.

Nick ran his fingers through his hair. More blood. Smeared all over.

"What happened to you?" Woong asked.

"Go find your mom." Nick wasn't looking at either of them. He was panting. Totally out of breath. "Find your mom, and tell her it's an emergency. Hurry."

Woong shrugged and darted off.

Kennedy kept staring, but at least now she'd found her voice. "What happened?"

Nick doubled over. For a minute, Kennedy thought he was going to be sick. "There's blood everywhere. It's …" He swayed, and Kennedy had to put her arm under him to keep him from crashing.

She lowered him to the ground. His face was ashen, a grayish pallor. Sweat beaded on his forehead.

He shook his head, smeared with blood. "Everywhere," he repeated in a whisper.

What was it? An accident? Did one of the teens get hurt? Kennedy lowered her face to his, trying to snap his brain to attention. "What is it?"

He held his head in his hands. "I tried to stop the bleeding. I tried to call for help."

"Help with what? Who's hurt?"

Nick let out a sigh. His whole body reeked. She knew people could get nauseated at the sight of blood, but she didn't know they started to smell bad, too.

"Carl." Nick blinked. "He's unconscious."

CHAPTER 4

By the time Kennedy left Nick in his puddle of queasy nerves and ran to Carl's office, Sandy was rushing down the hall from the opposite direction. "What is it, honey?" she asked Kennedy, breathless.

"Carl." Kennedy could barely get the word out.

Sandy rushed into the room, and Kennedy followed right after. Nick hadn't exaggerated. Apparently, neither had Woong. One of the bookshelves was toppled over, leaning precariously against the desk. Carl was on the floor at a painfully awkward angle, blood pooling beneath him.

Sandy dropped to her knees and scooped his head into her lap. "Carl? Darling? Can you hear me?" Her eyes were wide, but her voice held no trace of the panic and fear that gripped Kennedy's heart. "Sweetheart? Do we need to call you an ambulance?"

Sandy glanced over and looked at Kennedy. "Do you have your phone on you, dear?"

Kennedy reached into her pocket. Had she been stupid enough to leave it in her backpack at a time like this? No, there it was. Thank God. "I've got it."

She had already started dialing 911 when Sandy said, "Call the paramedics. Let them know he's a diabetic. I wonder if something went wrong with his medicine. He was supposed to eat his lunch, but he's been so busy getting everything ready for this conference, and he's … oh, my poor, precious darling." She stroked his cheek with the back of her hand. Either she didn't notice or didn't care that her dress was stained. Kennedy tried to figure out where he was bleeding from but couldn't tell from her vantage point. Were there any gloves in the area? Anything sterile?

Sandy kept stroking his cheek, crooning softly.

"Please state the location of the emergency." Thankfully this dispatcher, unlike others she'd been forced to talk to in the past, sounded more like a human than a robot.

"I'm at St. Margaret's Church on Elm Street. We need medical care. Our pastor here's bleeding. We don't know what happened."

"Is the patient conscious?"

"No. He's lying on the floor. There's a big pool of blood, maybe nine inches in diameter. Maybe more."

"Is he breathing?"

Kennedy stopped. Why hadn't she thought to check? She stared at his chest. "Yes, he's breathing." Praise the Lord.

"And the source of the bleeding?" the dispatcher asked.

"Don't forget to tell them about the diabetes," Sandy interrupted. "He took his insulin a full hour and a half ago."

Kennedy had a hard time keeping up two conversations at the same time, especially with her heart racing so fast and her lungs threatening to close in on her.

"I think it's from his head. It's hard to tell." She glanced at Sandy's dress. Was the blood continuing to pool on her lap?

"Don't forget …" Sandy began.

"He's got diabetes," Kennedy blurted.

"Is he on any medications?" the dispatcher asked.

Kennedy's lips quivered, but thankfully her voice remained steady. "He takes insulin. I don't know what else. But his wife is here. She could tell you." She held out the phone to Sandy. "Do you mind answering a few of their questions?"

"Of course not." She took the phone with a dignified kind of grace. "This is Sandy Lindgren speaking."

Kennedy didn't listen to the rest of the conversation. She tried to remember what other basic first-aid measures she should take while they waited for the ambulance. Slow down the bleeding. That was the first priority. But how? And with what? She didn't even know where he'd been injured. Something Woong said ran through her mind. *A real, actual fight. Like in those Jackie Chan movies.* It couldn't be that though. There had to be another explanation. Nobody would ever hurt Carl. Nobody …

She shoved those thoughts aside and opened his desk drawers. A devotional by different Puritan authors. Several folders filled with handwritten sermon notes. No first-aid kit anywhere.

"I don't think so." She heard Sandy's voice over the pulse raging in her ears. "His sugar was a little higher than normal this morning, something like 185 when he first woke up if I remember right. Or maybe that was last night. That's right. Last night was 185. This morning was 192. I told him he should take one of his pills, but he said he'd check it again after breakfast, except he always forgets …"

Kennedy searched through his desk. More journals. More books. Another drawer filled with nothing but photographs of his dozens of kids and grandkids.

"Oh, you know," Sandy went on as if she were chatting with a friend over tea. "The big white horse one. They're for diabetics. You'd recognize it if you saw it. Shaped like a long oval, have a little number on the side … no, I'm afraid I can't remember the name."

Kennedy wasn't sure if she would scream or pull her hair out. How could Sandy stay so calm in the midst of this madness? Even if Carl weren't hurt, his office was as chaotic as Murphy's Law itself. Books scattered everywhere. His bust of Charles Spurgeon had been knocked to the floor and now resembled an ancient ruin more than the nineteenth-century preacher. She knelt down and rummaged through the mess. At this point, she didn't even know what she was looking for. Medicine bottles so they could tell the paramedics exactly what Carl was taking? Gloves so she could check his injuries without risking infection? A church the size of St. Margaret's would have a first-aid kit somewhere. But wait. What was …

"The bleeding?" Sandy asked the dispatcher. "Well, let's see. I've got his head on my lap, and it looks like there's some blood on me now, so I wonder if maybe he got dizzy when his blood sugar dropped and fell and hit his head." She paused. "Well, I'm glad to hear that." She pulled the phone away from her ear and whispered to Kennedy, "The ambulance is only a few minutes away."

Kennedy stood frozen over the object she'd found. She didn't dare touch the thing but stared at it with a mix of both horror and incredulity. She tried to find the words to tell Sandy what she'd discovered.

"I'm sorry, what was that, dear?" Sandy asked.

Kennedy pointed to the heavy bookend. The bookend that was partially chipped and had bright red blood streaking across it.

"I said tell them to send the police, too. This might not have been an accident."

CHAPTER 5

Sandy shook her head while Kennedy helped her to her feet. "I can't believe someone would have done this on purpose."

The paramedics had just managed to get Carl onto the stretcher. Kennedy grimaced when she looked at him lying there. Her pastor was always so strong. Confident. But now he looked weak, and it wasn't because of the extra weight he'd recently lost. One eye was starting to swell. Cuts and scrapes streaked across his face. His hair was matted with dried blood, but at least he wasn't bleeding as much as at first.

"Nobody had any reason to do this," Sandy whispered.

Kennedy wrapped her arm around her shoulders, doing her best to ignore the stains on Sandy's clothes. "Don't worry about that right now. What matters is the ambulance is here, and they're going to get Carl the care he needs."

"He's such a good man." Sandy's voice caught. "Such an honest, godly man. Who would want to hurt him?"

Kennedy wished she could say it was still unclear if somebody had hurt him or not, but that wasn't the case. After taking one look at the scene, the first responder had radioed in to confirm that this was an attack. The police were on their way, and everyone at the church was ordered to remain on the premises. The officers would want to ask questions. Try to figure out what happened, who would have hurt someone as loving as Carl.

"Will you be following us in your car then, ma'am?" a first responder with thick glasses asked. "We're about ready to take your husband to Providence."

Sandy sniffed slightly and tucked her braid over her shoulder. Unruly strands of gray hair hung in sweaty clumps around her forehead. She smoothed out her dress. "I'm not leaving him. I'll go with you."

The paramedic glanced at one of his partners who shrugged. "It's all right with me. She can give us a better medical history on the way."

Sandy tilted up her chin. "Thank you. I just need to find my son."

The paramedic cleared his throat. "I'm sorry, we don't have that kind of room. If you two want to follow us to the hospital in your own vehicle, that would definitely be …"

"I can drive Woong," Kennedy offered.

"Mom?" The high-pitched voice in the doorway made Kennedy start.

"Oh, my baby." Sandy rushed toward Woong and hugged him while he made a valiant effort to squirm free.

"What's going on?" he asked. "Someone told me Dad got hurt, but I knew he must be lying because Dad wouldn't …" Woong stopped when Sandy moved him out of the way to make room for the two men transporting the stretcher. "Holy macaroni." Woong's face scrunched up. "What's wrong with Dad?"

"Shh." Sandy buried her cheek against his hair. "It's all right, son. Daddy had a little accident, and these nice folks are going to take him to the hospital so they can make him all better. Would you like to ride with Daddy in the ambulance, son?"

The paramedic cleared his throat. "I'm afraid there won't be room for both of you, but you're welcome to follow us and meet us at the …"

Sandy shook her head and stared down at him. "That man you're transporting is the father of my son. He's his only living male relative he's got left in this world, at least so far as we know. And so I'm going to tell you again. We are going to ride to the hospital with his father. Together."

He shook his head. "Not gonna work. I'm sorry. We'll

need all the space we can get, and if something happens in transit …"

"Like what?" Sandy interrupted. "What would you expect to happen? What could go wrong now?"

Kennedy was busy studying Woong's scrunched-up face and put her arm around Sandy. "Let me drive you, ok? It's the least I can do to help."

Sandy hadn't taken her eyes off her husband.

"It will be all right," Kennedy whispered, hoping she was speaking the truth. "Come on. You and Woong get your things ready, and I'll meet you at your car. Do you know where the keys are?"

"Carl usually keeps them in his pocket." Sandy's voice trembled.

After a quick explanation and a little help from the paramedics, Sandy took the car keys from Carl's pants and handed them to Kennedy. "I can drive myself, you know. You don't have to do this."

"I know." Kennedy offered what she hoped was a reassuring smile. "But I want to. Just think of it as a thank you for all the ways you've been there for me in the past, all right?"

Sandy frowned. "Ok. I'll meet you at the Honda. It's in the usual spot." She gave Kennedy a quick hug and turned to her son. "Woong, honey, do you have anything you need to take with you? Did you finish that math assignment I gave you earlier?"

Kennedy slipped out while Woong gave an excuse about losing his workbook. She had to find Willow. Had to tell her that she was driving Sandy and Woong to Providence.

Had to tell Willow about Carl's brutal attack.

CHAPTER 6

By the time Sandy and Woong emerged from the church, Carl's ambulance had already left. Kennedy knew there was no way to keep up with an emergency response vehicle with its sirens on, but she still wanted to get Sandy and Woong to Providence as soon as she safely could. She was glad for the chance to drive the two of them. Not only did it give her something practical to do, a tangible way to help in this horrific crisis, it would also mean she'd get the most recent updates on Carl's condition. She couldn't imagine having to sit and wait at St. Margaret's wondering about Carl.

The paramedics had worked professionally and efficiently to prepare Carl for transfer. Nobody gave Sandy much of a prognosis, at least nothing more than the fact that he was stable enough to transport to the hospital, but Kennedy had picked up on enough nonverbal cues to fear that Carl was going to need more than some stitches and Band-Aids once he got to Providence.

Or maybe she was just being paranoid. It was a bad

semester for someone she loved to get a head wound, given the fact that her neuroscience class was basically a crash course in the scariest, most horrifying types of brain injuries and abnormalities known to modern science. If you were a student reading a textbook or listening to your professor's lecture, the subject matter was fascinating. If you were a young woman driving your worried friend and her scared-silent son to the hospital after her husband suffered some kind of traumatic head injury, it was a curse. Kennedy's mind reeled with all the knowledge she'd gained, with all the worst-case scenarios floating around in her memory banks. It was one of those moments when ignorance could easily be compared to bliss.

Carl's favorite local talk show was on the AM radio. The host was yelling angrily about the protests and marches feminists had planned against St. Margaret's if the church didn't cancel the Truth Warriors conference.

"What is it that's so offensive to these feminists with their combat boots and camo pants, huh? What's so threatening about a religious event whose primary goal — in fact, its only stated goal — was to teach men to be more humble, compassionate defenders of the faith? I've got feminist leader Sandra Green in the studio with me, and I know I, as well as many of you, would love to hear her answer to these questions."

"Well, Chris, here's what I have to say to that." Sandra's voice was low and scratchy, like a woman who'd chain-smoked for half a century. "We certainly have no problem encouraging compassion and humility in a Judeo-Christian setting. Even a gathering that intentionally excluded women wouldn't be considered *threatening* as you put it if that was all there was to it. In other words, it's not the stated goals of the conference that are troublesome. It's the undertone, the subtext. The Truth Warriors movement assumes that anyone on this planet who presents as male has some type of divine right, some manifest destiny to subdue and subjugate anyone and everyone who presents as female. That's what we find so disturbing. That's why we urge anyone who …"

Kennedy turned the radio off. When she stopped at a red light, she glanced over at Sandy. "Are you doing ok?"

Sandy nodded but her lip was trembling. She turned around to look at her son. "How about you, darling? Are you still my big, brave baby?"

In the rearview mirror, Kennedy saw Woong scowl and cross his arms. "I'm not a baby," he mumbled, "and I've never been scared a day in my life."

Kennedy tried to think of something to say. Sandy was always so good in situations like these. Always had the right words, the right encouragement. But now, Kennedy felt about as lost as all those boys in *Lord of the Flies* right after they crash-landed on their deserted island.

"Well, honey, have you been praying for your daddy?" Sandy asked Woong.

"Yes," he grumbled from the backseat.

"Let's do it out loud this time. It'll make Daddy happy to know that we've been talking to God about him, and if the injuries are real serious ..." Her voice caught, and she coughed quietly.

"If the injuries are serious," Kennedy finished for her, "our prayers can help him recover faster."

"Yeah, whatever," Woong mumbled.

Kennedy figured it was time to jump in instead of passively wait for Sandy to have a teaching moment with her son. "You shouldn't talk about prayer that way," Kennedy told him. "Don't you remember when you got so sick last spring? It was God who helped you get better, you know."

"No it wasn't. It was the doctors. If it was God who healed me, he woulda done it without having to put that medicine in my arm that burned every time they made it drip into my blood."

Kennedy realized that she probably wasn't in the right emotional state of mind to dive headfirst into a theological landmine with an inquisitive boy like Woong.

"Well," she tried again, "sometimes God uses doctors, and sometimes he uses miracles, but that doesn't mean we shouldn't pray because prayer always makes a difference even if we don't always see what that difference is."

Even as the words came out of her mouth, Kennedy realized they lacked both conviction as well as common sense. Hadn't she learned, hadn't she matured enough to realize that those sorts of pat answers kids hear in Sunday school do nothing to prepare them for the trials and uncertainties of life?

But what else could she say?

Apparently, Woong's brain was working at least as fast as hers and dissecting her haphazard arguments as quickly as she was able to voice them.

"So you're saying God might make my dad get better if I pray, but he might not. And maybe he'll do it by some miracle, or he might just let the doctors do what they're supposed to do anyway. So what's the point of talking to Jesus about anything at all if he's already got his old, stubborn mind made up?"

"Woong," Sandy snapped and turned around in her seat. "You don't ever talk about our Lord and Savior that way, you understand me, child? If your dad were here and he heard you talk about his precious Jesus like that, what do you think he'd …"

"Well, Dad's not here." Woong answered back with just as much vehemence in his squeaky, little voice. "He can't hear me say things like that because … because …" He sniffed loudly and tried to choke down a small sob.

Sandy let out her breath. "Oh, my sweet baby, it's ok to be sad. It's ok to be worried about Daddy. I'm worried too, son."

Woong was crying softly with his fists balled up against his eyes.

"It's ok, little pumpkin," Sandy crooned and then began to pray. "Oh, dear sweet Jesus, comfort to all who mourn, protector of all the weak, the one who grants peace and courage to the scared and helpless, you are my King. You are my shield and my fortress and my salvation. You are the stronghold of my life. But I confess that even though I know these things about you, I don't worship you the way I should. I'm so frail, so easily given to fear. But I will yet praise you, my Savior and my God, feeble though my worship is. I bring it to you, Lord, all of it. The fears, the doubts, the dread. Father, you know just what's going on in my Carl's body. You know exactly what needs to be fixed, and you know exactly how to do it. So go now and heal him, Lord Jesus, please. As much as we might try to be brave, the truth of the matter is that Woong and I just wouldn't know how to live without that man. So go be with him now, Lord. And while you're healing all his wounds, come and fill us up in this car with your presence, too. Fill us up with the joy of your salvation, the joy that comes from knowing that neither death nor life, neither the past nor future, neither angels nor demons can separate any one of us from your perfect, eternal love. We ask this all in Jesus' name, and we give you all the glory and power and praise. Amen."

Sandy reached back and rubbed Woong's knee. Kennedy couldn't tell if he was still crying or not. She didn't hear anything, but she had to keep her eyes on the road as she pulled in front of Providence Hospital.

"Do you want me to drop you off at the entrance and Woong and I can come find you after we park?" Kennedy asked.

Sandy stared out her window. "What's that? Did you say something, sweetie?"

Kennedy repeated herself.

"That sounds like a good idea." Sandy still hadn't answered the question, but Kennedy assumed she meant that she wanted to be dropped off. She pulled the Lindgrens' Honda in front of the emergency room exit.

"Woong and I will be right behind you." Kennedy gave Sandy's hand a squeeze before she got out. "And I'll be praying for you. I'm sure Carl's going to be just fine."

Sandy frowned and said in a whisper only Kennedy could hear, "I wish I could be so sure of that myself. I've got a bad feeling about this."

CHAPTER 7

"Why does everybody who gets sick go to the same hospital?" Woong asked once Kennedy parked.

"What do you mean?" She got out and opened Woong's door so he wouldn't bang it against the cement pillar in the parking garage.

"What I mean is folks at hospitals are getting all kinds of different germs, so why don't they have one hospital for all the broken bones, and one hospital for all them folks with diabetes, and some other spot for the ones having their baby and so on?"

Kennedy locked the doors to the Honda and had to remind herself that Woong was too big to hold her hand. "That's a good question. I guess it's just easier having everything all together, so if the doctors need to give the patients X-rays or something it's all right there."

"Yeah, but I've been thinking, and now what I'm wanting to know is how come when all the bad stuff happens it always starts with folks coming here to the hospital or ending up here?"

"It does seem like that's the case, doesn't it?" Kennedy was glad she found a spot not too far from the entrance. She wasn't sure she had the patience for Woong's version of twenty thousand questions.

"Know what else I'm wondering?" he asked as they made their way to the sky bridge that connected the parking garage to the main building.

"What's that?" Kennedy was prepared for anything from a theological discussion about the possibility of extraterrestrial life to an observation about the mating rituals of the giraffes at the zoo.

"What I've been wanting to know is how come Mom got mad at me in the car? I wasn't trying to be disrespectful to God or stuff and nonsense like that. I really wanted to know."

Kennedy had been so worried about Carl's condition she couldn't remember exactly what Woong had said or done.

"Because I've been thinking," he went on, "and what I'm wondering is how come we're supposed to pray that God's gonna heal my dad, only if he doesn't, we're supposed to just say, *Ok, that must not have been the thing God wanted to do.* Because what I'm saying is if God's gonna do what God's gonna do, then why should we have to pray about it so hard, know what I mean?"

Kennedy was having a difficult time focusing. She still wasn't sure if these occasional bursts of mental fog were one of the side effects from her anxiety meds or just a sign of the anxiety itself. One thing she'd learned over the past two years was that as soon as she felt like she'd gotten the upper hand on one of her PTSD symptoms, another one — just as bad or sometimes even worse — was waiting in line, ready to move to the forefront.

"And here's the other thing," Woong said as they got onto the elevator to the main lobby. "Don't you think it'd make God mad if we ask him to heal a Christian? What I mean is don't all the Bible books and all the pastors say that it's better in heaven than it is on earth? And wouldn't God know that so wouldn't he want a Christian to go to heaven and be happy forever? So when we pray like Mom did for God to heal folks that are saved, what's keeping him from getting angry at us for being selfish-like?"

Kennedy knew that this wasn't a question she could brush off like the others. "First of all, God tells us we can talk to him about anything. And it's not selfish to want to keep from losing somebody we love. Jesus cried when his friend Lazarus died, even though he knew he was going to raise him back to life. But even more important, nobody's talking about your dad going to heaven. Lots of people have to ride in ambulances, but that doesn't mean they're so sick or hurt you have to worry about them dying."

Woong didn't respond. They got off the elevator, and Kennedy led him toward the ER. She'd been to Providence so many times by now there was no need to ask the volunteer behind the welcome desk for directions.

"Come on, bud. Let's find your mom and dad and then you'll see that there's no reason to think about anyone going off to heaven."

Even as she said the words, Kennedy prayed that she was right.

CHAPTER 8

Kennedy stared at her phone when it rang at her. It was a local number, but it wasn't in her contacts list. "Hello?"

"Hi, I'm calling from the T station. Can you hear me?" The voice was familiar, but she couldn't place it.

"Yeah. Who's this?" She'd only been in the ER waiting room for a short time. Sandy had come to take Woong back with her a few minutes earlier. At that point, there was still no word on Carl's condition.

"It's me. Ian."

"Who?"

"Ian. Ian McAlister."

"Oh." Kennedy pictured the journalist with his shock-red hair. She couldn't remember how long it had been since she'd last spoken with him. Over a year probably. Why would he be calling her?

"Hey, I wanted to talk to you about something. Is now a good time?"

Ian was the kind of journalist who seemed to know every

local headline a second or two before it happened. Had he already heard about Carl's attack? Kennedy wouldn't be too surprised to find out he knew even more than she did, although she could never guess who his sources were or how he got his information.

"I've got a couple minutes. Not very long."

"I understand. You getting ready for a class?" Ian's voice was casual, but the familiarity in his tone made Kennedy uneasy.

"No. I'm, well, I'm at the hospital with a friend."

"Oh, I'm sorry to hear that. Nothing too serious, I hope?" He sounded polite without being pushy.

"I hope not, too." Kennedy didn't want to give him any further details.

There was an awkward pause before he went on. "Well, I guess now's probably not the best time to talk then, but I wanted to sit down with you to discuss your article that came out today."

"What article?" Kennedy wondered if he'd called the wrong number. Did he think he was talking to someone else, maybe?

The roar of a passing T car in the background made Ian shout. "The one in the Harvard Voice. Your column on the feminist movement."

"Oh. That." Last week, the staff of the Voice had published an op-ed about the Truth Warriors conference at St. Margaret's. It was the same bandwagon every other liberal news outlet in Cambridge had jumped on. *Let's complain about the pastor who hosts a conference for men to talk about male leadership in the home and church.*

The only reason Kennedy wrote back to the editorial team was because they had personally attacked Sandy. In their editorial, they made her out to be some beaten-down housewife married to this megalomaniacal pastor who wanted to keep her barefoot in the kitchen and a perpetual slave to a never-ending line of children and grandchildren. Kennedy wrote a short email, no more than three or four sentences long, defending her friend and almost immediately received an invitation to print a seven-hundred-word rebuttal in the forum section of the Voice. So much had happened between now and then that she hadn't even realized her article had gone to print.

"It's caused quite a stir on campus from what I can tell. Which maybe is what you had in mind." Was Ian accusing her? His tone was indecipherable.

"No, I just wanted to see them treat Sandy better in the future."

His voice softened. "I can respect that. Their original article did hit a little below the belt if you want my opinion."

Kennedy waited. She still couldn't figure out why the journalist was calling her. Ian had graduated from Harvard years ago. Why did he care what students there did or didn't print in the paper?

"Anyway, I wanted to know if I could ask you a few questions. Maybe get your take on what it's like to be a conservative student on a campus like Harvard. It can't be easy, I'm sure."

Kennedy didn't know what to say. She'd never considered herself all that conservative before, especially not compared to people like Carl or her dad. Up until now, she hadn't even felt like her column for the Voice was taking a political side one way or the other. She just wanted to point out that Sandy did a whole lot more than sit around darning socks for her husband like the Harvard editors insinuated.

Kennedy's phone beeped at her. Willow was calling.

"You know what," she said, "I've got to run. There's a lot going on right now, but maybe we can talk soon."

"Breakfast tomorrow?"

Kennedy was fumbling with her phone, trying to disconnect with Ian before Willow hung up. "Ok, maybe." She ended the call before either of them could say good-bye and hoped that she hadn't missed her roommate. "Willow? Hello? Are you there?"

No response.

"Can you hear me?" she asked.

Was that someone sniffling?

"Willow? What's wrong?"

She let out a small sob.

Kennedy's abs tightened, and the all familiar quivering returned to her gut. "What happened? What's the matter?"

"It's Nick. The detective came to ask him what he knows about Carl's accident." It took a few sniffs and another suppressed sob before she could continue. "They think he's the one who attacked Carl."

CHAPTER 9

Kennedy had to stand up. Had to move her legs. She paced back and forth along the far wall of the ER waiting room where she hoped not too many patients and visitors could overhear. "What do you mean they think Nick did it? That's ridiculous." She tested her words, surprised they didn't come out a little more forcefully.

"I know, but everyone heard them fighting. That's the thing. And that dumb detective doesn't know him. He doesn't care. I tried explaining to him that Nick and Carl have fought for years and never once did it turn violent, but he was all like, *I'll question you if I've got any time after I'm finished with your boyfriend,* and he just lifted his little coffee cup in my face and basically told me where to go."

Coffee cup? That sounded familiar. "Is it Drisklay?" Kennedy asked.

"Is what drizzling? Outside? No, it's been perfectly clear all day."

"No, I mean the detective. Is his name Drisklay?"

"I don't know." Willow's voice was agitated, but at least she wasn't crying anymore. "His name could be Tutankhamen for all I care. I just want him to leave Nick out of this. He had nothing to do with any of it. Everyone knows that."

Kennedy believed her, but she also had to admit that with as loudly as Nick had been arguing with Carl, it would be amiss for the detective to fail to at least ask him a few standard questions. She thought about how bloody his hands were when he stumbled down the hallway of St. Margaret's.

"What should we do?" Willow asked softly.

"Just try not to worry for one thing. Drisklay's a pain, but he's not an idiot. He'll question Nick, and he'll do a thorough enough job that it'll be obvious he didn't have anything to do with the accident. And then you can talk to the detective yourself and tell him the same thing. Nick and Carl fight all the time. Everyone who spends more than five minutes at St. Margaret's knows that."

Kennedy was trying to lighten the mood, but Willow didn't laugh.

"I just hate thinking of him in there being treated like some terrorist suspect or something …"

"That's not what's happening. It's going to be all right.

Drisklay's just doing his job. It's not personal, and Nick has absolutely nothing to worry about."

"You sure?" Willow sounded so hopeful. So trusting.

Kennedy took a deep breath. "Yeah. I'm sure. This will all blow over. You'll see."

Willow sighed. "I hope so. What's the news on Carl?"

"No news yet." Kennedy checked the time. It hadn't even been ten minutes since she arrived.

"Well, you know we're all praying for him. We got the whole youth group together. All the teens and the helpers, and we spent our time in the sanctuary praying for Carl. You should have been there. It was really special."

Kennedy's throat was sore. "I bet it was."

"You doing ok? Not feeling too anxious or anything? I mean, of course we're all nervous, but you know what I'm saying."

"No panic attacks," Kennedy told her, deciding to take the direct approach to Willow's question. "Nothing like that." Maybe her pills really were helping. She thought about what she and Woong had talked about, how sometimes God heals people through miracles and sometimes through medicine. It still counted as healing because it still came from God, right?

She shouldn't feel guilty, should she?

"Kennedy!"

She turned at the sound of the voice from the opposite side of the lobby. "I better go," she told Willow. "Sandy's here."

"Let me know what you find out," Willow said. "The worst part is just waiting around like this."

"I know. I'll be sure to call you right back or at least send you a text. Gotta run." Kennedy ended the call, disappointed to find she only had one-and-a-half bars of battery life left. She didn't think she'd been talking that long, but it didn't matter. She hurried over to Sandy and Woong. "What's going on?"

Sandy's face was calm and serene, but her voice trembled. "Well, we've got some good news, and we've got some bad news."

Kennedy braced herself.

Sandy kept Woong pressed against her side, only this time he didn't try to squirm away but rested his cheek against her side, hiding part of his face in the folds of her dress. Sandy cleared her throat. "So, the good news is we got him here so fast, and the ambulance crew did such a good job tending to him on the road. He really couldn't have received any better care."

Sandy's use of the past tense sent Kennedy's whole body into a dizzying spiral.

"I better sit down." Sandy scooped Woong onto her lap and buried him against her shoulder. He didn't pull away.

Kennedy had no recollection of moving but realized she was sitting down now, too.

Sandy stroked Woong's head with one hand and wiped her cheek with the other. "It's harder than I thought it would be to say this."

Kennedy's throat was almost entirely swollen shut or she would have found some way to offer Sandy a word of comfort or encouragement.

Sandy sniffed and continued to caress her son. "By the time the ambulance got him here, Carl had stopped breathing. The man I talked to wasn't sure why. Said it might be from blood loss or maybe something like shock." She cleared her throat again and lowered her voice. "He said it might also be the result of brain injury. They won't know more until they run some tests, but they're getting him hooked up to life support. Or maybe they've finished by now. I didn't ask how long it would take."

"Did you get to see him?" Kennedy asked.

Sandy shook her head. "No, this is all from the paramedic I talked to, one of the ambulance crew. He's the one who let me know about how he stopped breathing on the road. Those folks saved your daddy's life." She spoke into

Woong's head of black hair. "We've got to remember to thank God for them every single day. You listening to me?"

Woong nodded but kept his face hidden.

Kennedy reached out and touched Sandy's arm. "What can I do?" she asked. She couldn't remember any time all year when she'd felt so helpless.

Sandy grabbed hold of her hand. "You can pray with me. And we've got to pray hard."

CHAPTER 10

Kennedy had never spent so long praying for one person before. She'd always had a nagging suspicion that interceding for others was a lot harder than certain pastors and Bible study leaders made it out to be. Even so, she never guessed how exhausting it was to spend that much time in focused, fervent prayer. Kennedy figured they'd prayed at least forty-five minutes and maybe a whole hour, interrupted only a few short times when the nurse popped out to let Sandy know what was happening. Carl's condition hadn't changed. Once he got stabilized on the ventilator, the doctor wanted to monitor him for a little while longer in the ER and then send him to the ICU. Sandy took the news with her typical grace, but Kennedy wanted to jump up and scream to the entire hospital that it wasn't fair.

Carl shouldn't be here. He shouldn't be on a ventilator. He couldn't be. He was so strong. It wasn't as bad as the nurse made it out. It just wasn't possible.

And each time the nurse left, Sandy would invite Kennedy again to pray. Woong had gotten past his clingy stage and was antsy, so Kennedy showed him how to play Scrabble on her phone. The battery died just a minute before they ended their prayer. If it hadn't, she had a feeling Sandy could have gone on for another full hour of devoted intercession. As it was, the fact that her phone battery held its charge for even that long was some small miracle, or at the very least an unusual and unexpected blessing.

Sandy stroked Kennedy's arm and smiled gently at her. "Thank you for praying with me, sweetheart. It did my soul a world of good."

"I'm glad to hear that." Kennedy was trying to guess if the softness in Sandy's features was just her regular, warm expression, or if she really did look different after their time in prayer together.

Sandy stood up with a quiet groan. "I guess I'd better go ask the nurse if there's any news. Maybe we can go back and see him soon."

Kennedy was afraid Sandy would ask her to come, too. Of course, she'd go if that's what Sandy wanted, but the thought of seeing Carl so weak, laying there paralyzed with a machine doing all his breathing for him, made Kennedy feel like she was about to suffocate.

Brain damage? Not someone like Carl. God wouldn't let something happen that was so senseless. Such a waste. And because of what? Some hoodlum? Who would attack a person like Carl? Who would want to hurt him? All he did was love people. Love people, take strangers into his home, and share the gospel with everyone around him. Not the type of guy you'd expect to be walking around with a target sign on the back of his head reading *attack me.*

Kennedy squeezed her eyes shut. There was no energy left to ask God for anything. She just had to trust that he had heard her prayers earlier. Now all she could do was wait. Wait and try to offer Sandy some moral support. Woong, too. He'd been pouting ever since the phone battery died, but he was too old to play with the little toddler toys, and there was nothing else in the waiting room but magazines and TVs.

While Sandy went to talk to the nurse, something on one of the screens caught her eye. It was a scene from Harvard right outside the student center. She blinked so her contacts wouldn't be so dry and tried to focus on the small words. She'd have to stand up. Just as well. It was time to give her legs a stretch anyway.

"I'll be right back," she told Woong and walked closer to the television.

"Harvard administration is trying to track down the culprits responsible for a slew of graffiti incidents across campus. It seems as if the attack is a backlash to a conservative newspaper article printed in the student paper, the Voice, in which a Harvard junior defends the traditional role of the stay-at-home mother."

Kennedy stared at the screen with the same undivided attention as the fire chief in *Fahrenheit 451* hunting down books to burn.

The camera switched to a shot of the outside of her dorm room, where ugly green graffiti sported a quote Kennedy recognized from her column. She wasn't listening to the news anchor anymore. All she could hear was her pulse pounding in her ears. It was too much. Carl so badly injured, and now the entire campus was angry at her for daring to suggest some women might prefer to raise kids instead of chasing a career?

She pressed her fingers against her temples. She had a throbbing headache. Who cared if the anxiety meds kept her from having so many panic attacks if she had to put up with a migraine whenever she got stressed?

This was too much. Too much for her to focus on. It didn't matter if someone hadn't liked her article. The editor of the forum section had already warned her about that. She wasn't on campus right now. Who cared what people said? It wasn't like they were attacking her personally. They were just attacking her choice of words.

She glanced once more at the screen, thankful to see Channel 2 had moved on to some other bit of news. It didn't matter what it was, as long as it wasn't about her.

Sandy had finished talking to the nurse and was with Woong. Kennedy returned to her seat, glad that her legs could still support her weight. "Any updates?" she asked.

Sandy straightened out the skirt of her dress, careful to avoid the bloody spots. "Well, they hooked him up to the ventilator without any problems. That's a good thing. I was just asking Woong if he wanted to go back and see his daddy. I told him it'd be a little strange. There'll be tubes and things since Daddy's on the machine that's helping him with his breathing."

"I can stay here with Woong," Kennedy suggested. She couldn't picture any scenario in which it'd be beneficial for a young boy like Woong to see his father in such a state, at least not until he had more time to get used to the idea.

Or until it started to look like Carl would be on the ventilator indefinitely.

But no, that wouldn't happen. He was strong. His body was strong. His spirit was strong. Aside from the diabetes and a little extra weight, he was perfectly healthy. The ventilator was just a short-term solution to a problem that would correct itself in a few hours. A day or two max, and Carl would be better.

He had to be.

There was so much more work for the Lord he still had to do.

CHAPTER 11

"I'm bored," Woong announced as the afternoon wore on toward evening. "What's there to do?"

Kennedy sighed. "Want to go on a little walk?"

Woong rolled his head back and stared at the ceiling dramatically. "We've been on like ten walks already." The sad part was he probably wasn't exaggerating. He clutched his stomach. "I'm so hungry."

"If it's that bad, we could go get you a snack," Kennedy finally conceded. Woong had asked her at least a dozen times already, but with her phone dead she didn't want to be gone for too long in case Sandy came back out and wondered where they'd gone. The sun was due to set before long, and Kennedy had skipped lunch to catch the T to St. Margaret's earlier. She was just as ready to eat as Woong.

"We're not too far from the cafeteria," she said, "so if you pick something we can carry back here, I don't think it'll be a problem. We just have to hurry, all right?"

Woong beamed. "Do they have hot dogs?"

Kennedy picked up her backpack. "I don't know. Maybe."

"Holy macaroni!" Woong jumped out of his seat. It was refreshing to see his large grin back for a change.

"But remember we'll need to make up our minds really fast. And just one thing, not a whole bunch. I only have a little bit of cash on me."

"What's cash?" he asked.

"Coins and things. Dollar bills."

"Why don't you just use one of them credit cards like everyone else?"

Kennedy let out her breath. If it would keep Woong's mind off his father and his ventilator, she was willing to jump into another round of question and answers. Heaven knew she could use the mental distraction as well.

"Well, because …" She stopped when she spotted two familiar faces heading toward them.

"Kennedy!" Willow ran up in her sandals and threw her arms around her in a hug that in most cases would have been far too long for comfort. "I'm so glad we found you. I've been wicked anxious. I've been texting you all afternoon."

"I'm sorry. My battery …"

Willow rolled her eyes. "Don't say any more."

"Well, it wasn't entirely my fault this time."

Woong was suddenly twice as chipper as before. "Hi, Nick! We're about to get some food because I'm hungrier than a refrigerator."

Nick raised his eyebrows questioningly at Kennedy, but she wasn't able to explain the simile, either. Nick rubbed Woong's head. "That's cool. Maybe we'll join you then. Cafeteria's this way?"

Kennedy nodded. "Yeah, Sandy went back to see Carl a little while ago. We still haven't heard any updates or anything."

"He's on a ventilator now?" Willow asked in a low voice. Kennedy glanced at Woong, who was trying to beat Nick in a rock, paper, scissors game. She nodded.

"Dude," Willow exclaimed.

"I know what you mean," Kennedy replied.

"Dude."

"So," Nick interrupted with a smile, "are we getting a snack at the cafeteria or what?"

"Yeah." Willow rubbed Kennedy on the back. "Let's go."

They walked down the corridor, and Kennedy tried not to think about the last time she'd been led down this hall. The last hour she spent with Dominic. The months of painful mourning that followed.

Her Cape Cod vacation had been so good for her. It had been years since she and her parents had been in the States together. But all summer in that tiny little condo, she felt like the children in *Brave New World* paraded on display for everyone to examine. If she didn't sleep well, her mom clucked around and fretted about adjusting her prescription levels. If she didn't have an appetite, her dad would make her sit through an entire differential where he'd roll off several dozen symptoms and side effects he'd read about online. The worst was when her mom wanted to watch her sappy farm romances or historical sagas. If Kennedy couldn't conjure up the expected amount of warm fuzzies, if she gave even the slightest hint that she detested the predictable plots or clichéd dialog, her mom would assume Kennedy's reaction had to do with Dominic and berate herself for not being more sensitive in her choice of movies.

In fact, it seemed like her mom spent the entire summer hoping to make Kennedy forget all about Dominic. Erase him from her memory forever like the political dissidents in *1984*. Purged entirely until it was as if he'd never existed. Never asked Kennedy out on that first date. Never …

She couldn't set foot in Providence Hospital without thinking about him. There were reminders all around. She couldn't forget even if she wanted to. Which she didn't. The memories were painful, but they were a part of her now, just like the scars on her arm after what she'd gone through last spring. You could only cover yourself up with sweaters and turtlenecks for so long. Eventually you had to accept that the wounds were now just as much a part of you as your own DNA. Two things in life you can't escape — your genes and your past.

Woong ran ahead, chattering with Nick about his latest homeschool science experiment. Willow was still wearing her platform sandals, and she and Kennedy took a more leisurely pace.

"Looks like Nick's ok after the talk with the detective?" Kennedy asked.

"Yeah. I'm glad that got sorted out. For now, at least. The detective guy … what's his name again? Driscoll? Briskly?"

"Drisklay."

"Yeah, Drisklay. Whatever kind of name that is. He finished his interview with Nick. Didn't seem too bad. Nick wasn't worried. The detective will let him know if he has any other questions, but I think you were right. It was just a formality he had to go through." She let out a nervous chuckle. "I mean, who could seriously picture someone like

Nick going up against a retired football guy like Carl? The boy faints if you just talk about blood. You should have seen how pale he was before we got him cleaned up."

Kennedy did what she could to keep a positive outlook. "Well, it's good news he's off the suspect list. Do you think there are any other leads?"

Willow shrugged. "Drisklay or whatever his name is was already complaining about his coffee wearing off by the time he got to questioning me. I think he wrote me off as a biased witness anyway. I doubt we spent more than two minutes together, and I haven't heard anything else about the case so far. Speaking of cases, now might be a really bad time to mention it, but I don't want you to be caught off guard. Something happened back at the dorm."

"You mean the graffiti?"

Willow fingered the green tips of her hair. "Yeah. How'd you hear?"

"Saw it on Channel 2."

"Dude."

When they reached the cafeteria, Nick was already in line with Woong, who was trying to balance a whole tray of food stacked precariously high. So much for grabbing something quick and hurrying back to the ER to wait for news about Carl.

Willow gave Kennedy a comforting side hug. “I guess right now there’s more important things to worry about than what some fools thought of your newspaper article, right?”

Kennedy’s throat was parched, but she forced herself to swallow anyway. “Right.”

CHAPTER 12

Sandy was just coming out of the back rooms when Kennedy and her friends returned to the ER lobby. Woong ran up to her, apparently in a more congenial mood after Nick bought him two hotdogs, a bag of Cheetos, a big fruit salad ("on account of it having lots of good, healthy vitamins"), and a giant soft pretzel with double portions of melted cheese product.

Sandy bent over her son and gave him a hug. "How's my boy? Are you minding Miss Kennedy?"

Woong nodded. "I beat Nick at paper, scissors, rock," he boasted. "Except this is a new version. It's got a lizard and a funny alien guy with pointy ears who makes his fingers all funny." Woong tried to replicate the hand gesture.

Sandy looked clueless, but she brushed the stray hair out of her eyes and tried to offer everyone a smile. "Willow and Nick, it's good to see you both. How are you doing today?"

Nick stepped beside her and gave her a side hug. "What we really want to know is how's Carl? What have the doctors said?"

Sandy sat down and fidgeted with her skirt. It was a little bit wet. Kennedy wondered if she'd tried to wash some of the bloodstains out of it. Once everyone else was seated, Sandy put her arm around Woong and said, "Well, we have so much to thank the good Lord for. So much. Carl looks real peaceful back there." She sniffed and quickly wiped her cheek. "Real comfortable. And the doctors are confident that he's not in any kind of pain." She cleared her throat. "So right now, I'm counting that as a huge blessing. You know Carl and how much he hates hospitals." She let out a little chuckle that faltered unconvincingly at the end.

She paused for a moment and then resumed. "I guess the injury is a little more complicated than we might have hoped, but I'm convinced that through it all …" She held Woong a little closer, gave a weak smile, and tried again. "I'm convinced that through it all, God's purpose for my husband still stands. They'll be doing some brain scans before too long now, and after that we'll have a clearer picture of what his recovery might look like."

Nobody spoke. How was it possible? A few hours ago, Carl had been engaged in one of his favorite pastimes, debating politics with Nick, and now this? Brain scans, complicated recovery … what exactly was Sandy telling them?

Did Kennedy really want to know?

Willow was sitting across from Sandy and rested her hand on her knee. "You know Carl wouldn't want you to worry right now, don't you?"

Sandy nodded and wiped her cheeks again.

Kennedy watched her roommate's face for any sign of breaking. If Willow started to cry, then Kennedy would start to cry, and pretty soon they'd all be making a scene as loud and boisterous as the choir boys in *Lord of the Flies*.

Willow sniffed. It was going to happen. Kennedy couldn't stand the thought.

"Come on, guys." She infused artificial cheer into her voice. "Willow is right that this isn't how Carl would want us to react." Nods all around gave Kennedy encouragement. "He's always said that … He's never been afraid of anything, know what I mean? I don't think he'd want us to be afraid either." She forced a small chuckle. "In fact, we all can guess what Carl would be doing if one of us was on a ventilator and he was out here waiting for answers."

Woong sat up in his seat. "I know. He'd start praying, and he do it real loud-like on account of him being one of them sorts of Christians who don't care if other people laugh at them for talking to God in someplace besides church."

Instead of lightening the mood, Woong's words clawed and slashed at Kennedy's soul. *Why, God? Why would you put this family that loves you so much and has served you so faithfully through this kind of nightmare?* She looked over at Sandy, at the tears her friend was trying so hard to hide. Sandy had been there for dozens, no hundreds of hurting people over the years. Had rescued foster kids from lives of addiction and abuse, had prayed with the hurting, cried with the distraught. She was a pillar of strength, and an unshakable beacon of hope that so many had turned to during the storms in their lives.

And now it was time for somebody to offer her that same encouragement and love.

Kennedy couldn't remember if it was Willow or maybe Nick who suggested that they pray, or if they all just sensed the movement of the Holy Spirit and entered into God's throne room together out of some silent agreement. Even Woong sat perfectly still while prayers for Carl's healing and recovery were lifted up to the one who comforts the brokenhearted and binds up all their wounds.

CHAPTER 13

"So you'll call me if you hear anything about Carl, right?" Nick asked when he dropped Kennedy and Willow off on campus.

"Yeah. And you do the same if you get an update first." Willow gave him a light kiss and got out of his VW bus.

"You doing all right?" she asked Kennedy as they made their way toward their dorm.

Kennedy didn't know how to respond. How did you define *all right*? Was Willow talking about the panic attacks? In that case, yes, she felt fine. If anything, it seemed like she should be experiencing more inner turmoil than she was. Or maybe that was just the exhaustion. She and Willow had stayed at the hospital for several hours. Sandy made arrangements for Woong to spend the night with a friend from his former school, so after a quick dinner in the cafeteria, they'd gone with Nick to drop Woong off at the Linklaters' and had just now gotten back to Harvard.

Kennedy couldn't remember if she had any assignments

she'd have to work on before bed. Her first class wasn't until noon tomorrow, so maybe she should wait until morning. Was she ready for the next day's lab? Kennedy's former chemistry professor had hired her to TA the introductory chemistry lab, an honor for any undergrad, especially a junior. It was a little weird teaching students who were only two years younger than she was, but it was a fun challenge and reminded Kennedy how much she liked general chemistry. In fact, if she ever needed a fallback plan from med school, she could see herself going into the research side of things.

As humbled as she was to have been chosen as one of Adell's teaching assistants, right now she had other things to worry about besides the thirteen lab reports she couldn't remember if she'd finished grading or not. Oh, well. Even if she was too exhausted to get to it tonight, she'd have time in the morning. She'd find a way to make it work. She always did.

Willow slowed her pace as soon as their dorm came into view. At first Kennedy thought it was because of those high-heeled sandals, but then she saw the graffiti on the side of the building and remembered everything that happened on campus. The newspaper article. The angry students.

Willow glanced at her awkwardly. "You sure you're all right?"

Kennedy kept her eyes in front of her and refused to look at the graffitied wall. "I'm fine. It's just words. Words never hurt anybody." She didn't raise her eyes to Willow to try to guess if her roommate believed her or not.

Willow opened the door of the building, muttering something about closed-minded ignoramuses. Kennedy followed her into the dorm but stopped when someone behind her shouted her name.

"Kennedy! Hold up. I need to talk to you." The forum editor for the Voice ran up to her. O'Brien slipped inside, slightly out of breath. "I've been texting you all afternoon."

"My battery died."

O'Brien rolled his eyes. "Again?" He offered a small smile. "Well, it's a good thing I found you in time. The editors called together a meeting in five minutes. We need you there."

Kennedy did her best not to groan. "A meeting this late?"

He shoved his hands into his pockets. "Yeah, I know it might not be the most convenient, but this is pretty important."

"What's important," Willow interrupted, "is that you leave her alone. She's in the midst of a personal crisis here, and ..."

"That's why the editors called this meeting," he

answered. “It’s all because of that column you wrote, and since I’m the section head who signed off your article, we’re in this together whether you like it or not.”

Willow was about to reply, but Kennedy touched her on the arm. “It’s ok. You know there’s no way I could sleep now anyway. May as well go distract myself for a little bit. Don’t worry about me.”

Willow crossed her arms and jutted out her hip. “I am going to worry about you because you’re my best friend, and no one should have to be alone on a night like …”

“I won’t be alone.” Kennedy conjured up a smile and lowered her voice. “It’s all right. Trust me.”

“Fine,” Willow conceded, “but you give me your phone, and I’ll plug it in for you so if Sandy tries to get hold of you, I can pick it up.”

“Ok.” Kennedy took her phone out of her backpack and passed it to Willow.

“You sure you want to do this?” she whispered.

No, Kennedy wasn’t sure, but she didn’t have the energy to stand here arguing. She nodded. “Yeah. Like I said, it beats sitting around worrying.”

“Take care of yourself, hear?” Willow gave her a quick hug and whispered, “Don’t let anything they say get to you. You did the right thing publishing that article, and they have no right to bully you into feeling bad just for sharing an unpopular opinion."

Kennedy smiled, thankful to have a friend who took her well-being so seriously.

O'Brien, who'd been biting his lip and avoiding eye contact during Kennedy and Willow's exchange, held open the door. "So then, you ready?"

Kennedy nodded and adjusted her backpack. "I'm ready. Let's get this over with."

CHAPTER 14

Kennedy looked back once as she and O'Brien headed toward the student union building where the Voice held its offices. Willow was staring at her through the window of their dorm.

"She your bodyguard or something?" O'Brien asked.

"No, just my roommate."

O'Brien's hands were in his pockets, and his shoulders jutted up toward his ears. "I'm sorry I had to interrupt your night like this, especially if you've got other stuff going on." He jerked one ear toward his shoulder, making his neck vertebra crack.

Kennedy winced. "Don't worry about it. So what's this meeting all about?"

He wrenched his head the other way. More pops and creaks. "This is basically where you get chewed out for your antifeminist opinions, and I get slaughtered for allowing you to publish it in my section."

"You're joking, right?" Kennedy glanced at O'Brien,

who had taken his hands out of his pockets and was now cracking his knuckles.

"No. Perfectly serious. Happens once or twice a year, although I don't think we've had a case this big since President Reinholtz resigned."

"Who?"

"Reinholtz. The guy here the year before you came. You seriously didn't hear about him?"

Kennedy shook her head.

"Wow, you must have been living your entire college career in the dark. Reinholtz published a book citing all kinds of so-called scientific evidence that showed that male brains are different than female brains."

Kennedy hadn't realized you needed to be the president of an Ivy League school like Harvard to reach a conclusion like that, but by the way O'Brien was looking at her, she assumed he expected her to be shocked by the revelation.

"Then what?" she asked.

"What would you expect? The students, the staff, the media. They all crucified him. He resigned less than a month later. You're lucky you missed it. Things got really ugly."

"Because he said that men and women's brains are different?" Kennedy was still trying to figure out what the controversy was in the first place.

"Yeah. I mean, sure the guy's got a few screws loose to even publish garbage like that, but I guess I'm in the minority by thinking we could have actually heard his side and let him speak for himself instead of getting rid of him so fast. But anyway, all that to say you really touched a nerve with your article. I hate to sound smug, but I did try to warn you."

"I remember." Kennedy kept her voice low.

"So, this meeting, it's probably gonna be a little hostile in there, so I just want you to be prepared. Ok? Any questions?"

Kennedy didn't know where to begin. O'Brien had told her how unpopular her opinion would be when she submitted her column to the Voice, but that still hadn't prepared her for graffiti on her dorm or some kind of midnight inquisition where she'd have to defend herself before an entire panel of thought police.

She mentally rehearsed what she'd written in her column. She'd started off by saying that she knew Sandy Lindgren personally and was upset by the way the staff of the Harvard Voice had painted a woman they hadn't ever met in such a negative light simply because she was a stay-at-home mom and married to the man who had organized the Truth Warriors conference.

I'm not saying every woman has to stay home and take care of her family, Kennedy had written. *As a premed student eager to begin my career in medicine, I'm completely against women being denied a place in any academic or vocational field they feel drawn toward. But as a compassionate human being, I'm also against berating women whose life choices may be different than my own. There is nothing debasing or ignoble about a wife or mother who stays home to take care of her family* if that's what she chooses to do. *And it surprises me that a panel claiming to be as open-minded as the editorial staff of the Harvard Voice would malign an individual they've never met and make such a rash judgement call about her life and choices simply because she does not bring home a monthly paycheck.*

That was probably the most heated it got. Kennedy shook her head. She had more important things to do than explain herself to a bunch of students she didn't even know. Students who had most likely already labeled her a close-minded conservative after reading a simple, seven-hundred-word essay. She heard Carl in her head, voicing one of his go-to complaints: *It's like* 1984 *all over again.*

Maybe he was onto something there.

Thinking about Carl reminded her that she had a lot more serious problems to worry about than what some editors said about her silly piece of writing. She was glad Willow had taken her phone. Maybe by the time this interview was over, she'd get some news about Carl's prognosis. She still couldn't believe it was as serious as the doctors had told Sandy.

Actually, she could believe it, especially after all she'd read so far in her neuroscience class. The difference was this was her pastor, mentor, and friend, not some nameless case study in a text book. She'd known Carl since she was a tiny girl attending his church in Manhattan. She'd been half the size of Woong, or even smaller, when Sandy was her Sunday school teacher, when Carl would dress up as a clown or a cowboy or a zookeeper for each summer's theme-based vacation Bible school. Next to her dad, she loved Carl more than any other man in the world. The fear of having to say good-bye to him …

No, she couldn't think like that. After all God had dragged her through, losing Dominic and everything else that had happened over the past year or two, this would be too much. The Lord wouldn't ask her to give up Carl, too. She was overreacting. Leave it to her panic-prone imagination to exaggerate the situation. Carl was fine. His injuries were serious, but he'd recover by the grace of God and go back to the life and ministry he'd had before today's accident.

No, not accident. Attack. Why was it so hard to remember that?

The student union came into view, and Kennedy was tempted to feign a headache or concoct some other excuse to retreat. Actually, now that she thought about it, her head still hurt.

O'Brien opened the door, and they walked in. "Try not to take what they say personally, and let me do most of the talking, all right?"

Kennedy didn't answer but followed him up the stairs that led to the Voice office.

O'Brien rolled his shoulders and popped his back. "Ok." He led the way into the editorial room. "Let's do this."

CHAPTER 15

Kennedy stared at the faces around her, trying to figure out if there was anyone she recognized. She was initially surprised at how many staff members of the Voice were here. When O'Brien said she'd be meeting with the editors, she thought he meant the five section heads and the editor-in-chief, but apparently each section editor had an assistant who was also considered part of the staff, and there were also a few senior editors who no longer ran their own pages but still remained involved in the life and pulse of the Voice. Getting through the initial introductions took at least ten minutes.

Ten minutes Kennedy could have spent in her dorm room worrying about Carl. Or praying for him.

"Ok. Let's get to it." Marty, the editor-in-chief, unfolded that week's copy of the Voice. "I think we all know why we're here."

Kennedy didn't feel like now was the best time to point out Marty's mistake.

O'Brien cleared his throat. "I just want to take a minute to point something out before we begin."

Great. Now was the time when he'd say that he had absolutely nothing to do with Kennedy's column.

Marty nodded at him, and he continued. "What I want to say is that I know the ideas in this column are troubling to a lot of us."

So much for his little *we're in this together* pep talk from earlier. Kennedy vowed to never write for publication again.

"But even if Kennedy's ideas are fairly unorthodox, I thought it would be an asset to the paper to present an opposing point of view. I read her article and found it to be a respectful, concise summary of the conservative viewpoint. That's why I allowed it to go to print."

Marty raised an eyebrow. Kennedy thought she recognized her but couldn't remember from where. One of her roommate's plays, maybe.

"So you're saying you stand by your decision to run this column?"

Kennedy held her breath.

O'Brien nodded. "Yes. That's absolutely what I'm saying."

There were quite a few murmurs around the table before Marty got everyone's attention again.

"All right. Thank you to O'Brien for his confirmation that he was not only involved but also gave full support to the opinions in this article."

O'Brien leaned forward in his chair. "Hold up. I didn't say I supported her opinions. I said I supported her right to make her opinions heard."

An assistant editor shook her head. "There's no difference. By giving her space in the paper, you're stating that you support her beliefs."

"That's not true. I gave her space in the paper because I believe that as open-minded individuals, like we all claim to be, we should give fair treatment to various sides of an issue."

"Not when that issue condones misogyny."

Kennedy's head swarmed while the editors bickered back and forth. There were so many different points being made by so many different people that she couldn't keep any of their arguments straight. It was clear, however, that O'Brien was the only one who thought Kennedy's article should have ever made it to print.

"We're a university that stands for free thought and open mindedness," he argued. "So what's it say about us when we silence anybody who doesn't believe what we do? Is it our job to pre-screen every single student's opinion and only publish what we agree with?"

"Of course," answered the news editor.

O'Brien shook his head. "Do you realize what you sound like? Aren't we supposed to be the open-minded ones in these debates? Aren't we the ones promoting tolerance and co-existence? Instead, we've become a mob eager to lynch anyone who …"

Marty coughed. "That's a problematic word right there. I'll need to ask you to change your language."

"What?" O'Brien looked around the table. "What'd I say?"

Marty rolled her eyes. "You said the word *lynch*, which for certain students from certain historical backgrounds carries an aggressive and threatening connotation."

Kennedy had kept her gaze low during the entire meeting. She didn't know if the fact that O'Brien was taking the entirety of the Voice staff's ire made her feel more guilty or relieved.

"So I can't say *lynched,* huh? It's yet another one of those words that have become offensive? What next? Are we going to force everyone here to start talking in newspeak?"

Several of the students looked confused, but Kennedy recognized the *1984* reference.

"What's next?" O'Brien continued. "We going to start blacking out words in the dictionary? Take a Sharpie and just smudge over them like they never existed?"

Marty shook her head. “I think we’ve all gotten a clear understanding of what you have to say. What if we have the writer speak for themself at this time?”

It wasn’t until all the faces around the table turned toward her that Kennedy realized who Marty was talking about. “Me?”

“Of course.” Marty smiled with false serenity. “It was your column that started this whole mess, and O’Brien’s right on one point. It would be wrong for us to do anything here tonight without giving you the chance to defend yourself. So go ahead. Tell us why women are supposed to stay at home and do nothing but raise babies. I’m sure we’re all dying to hear your opinion.” She shot O’Brien an angry glare.

Kennedy rubbed her sweaty palms against her jeans. “Ok.” She cleared her voice and tried to sneak a little confidence into her tone. “So, first of all, I never said that women should be forced to stay at home …”

“But you defended the pastor’s wife at that mega-church,” someone interrupted.

“Well, yeah, but I guess I see a difference between standing up for one individual and saying that every single person who happens to be a girl has to follow her example.”

“Female,” Marty inserted.

Kennedy didn't understand. "What's that?"

"Female," she repeated. "The term *girl* carries a derogatory tone. For example, you would never call someone who presents as male who's over the age of eighteen or twenty a boy, so why would you use the word *girl* when you're referring to an adult?"

Kennedy stared at the shiny boardroom table. "Ok, sorry about that. All I meant to say was when I wrote my piece I was trying to show that some females enjoy being stay-at-home moms, and if that's a choice they make, who are we to tell them it's wrong?"

"We're the progressive ones, that's who we are," Marty answered. "The ones on the right side of truth. Do you really think your little pastor's wife *enjoys* all that cooking she does every day?"

"Well, as a matter of fact …"

"And do you think," Marty interrupted, "that it's socially responsible to praise members of society who've given up all their own ambitions and dreams and career opportunities just so they can enslave themselves to their husbands and children?" She shook her head. "I read your article, and I see nothing but patriarchal propaganda. What about the case where a husband gets disabled and is unable to fulfill his traditional role as bread-winner? Is little Sally Homemaker supposed to smile and keep on baking him her casseroles and let their home get foreclosed? Or what about non-traditional couples, a trans male for example or two females in a monogamous relationship. Which one of them would be expected to stay home and take care of the babies in your perfect little world?"

Kennedy's palms were so wet she probably could have dried them on a paper towel and wrung it out afterward. "It wasn't my intention to dictate how every woman or female's supposed to behave. I just wanted to …"

"What I'm curious about," interrupted the editor sitting directly across from her, "is how you can justify investing so much time and energy and finances into a Harvard education just so you can find yourself some spouse and live happily ever after."

Kennedy glanced around the table. Several of the editors had been silent the entire meeting, but not even the quiet ones would raise their eyes to hers with anything but open hostility. She wondered what they would do if she simply announced she had lab reports to grade and got up and left. But what would that mean for O'Brien? He'd been right when he told her they were in this pit together. At the time, however, Kennedy had no idea how deep of a pit it would be.

"I'm not planning to be just a stay-at-home mom myself."

"Oh, really?" Marty grinned. "What other plans do you have? Selling cosmetics online?"

One of her dad's sayings ran through her head. *You shouldn't ever be surprised when a non-Christian fails to behave like a Christian.* Kennedy did her best to keep her voice calm so Marty couldn't sense her growing anger. "Actually, I'm going on to med school. I've already been accepted into Harvard's early admissions program."

Unfortunately, Marty didn't seem at all impressed. "So four years of med school and then what? Have a bunch of kids and babysit to pay off all your student loans?"

O'Brien cleared his throat. "This meeting isn't about Kennedy's future plans, or at least it shouldn't be. It's about her article. I think we'd save a lot of time and headache if we stuck to the original issue."

Marty shrugged. "I'm not so sure the two aren't more related than that. Tell me." She glowered at Kennedy. "What will you do if you find someone you want to marry only he doesn't want you to go to medical school? What then? Or what if you get pregnant before you graduate? Aren't all you conservatives against contraceptives? Then what? You're not going to have an abortion, and you can't strap a baby on your back while you're doing your surgical rounds. So what happens then?"

"What happens then," O'Brien boomed, "is irrelevant. This whole interrogation is pointless, but since we're here, let's focus on the matter at hand. Kennedy wrote an article. You guys don't like it because you disagree with what she had to say. So now what? You either fire her from submitting to the paper in the future, you come up with some opposing editorial, or you decide on something tangible to do. That's why we're here, not to talk about how her views on womanhood might complicate her career choice as a doctor. I personally would be happy to go to a practitioner who put a high priority on family life."

A black-haired girl in glasses smirked. "Yeah, unless she leaves you in the middle of an open-heart surgery because her preschooler's got a ballet recital."

Kennedy tried to clench her jaw shut, but even that wasn't enough to keep the torrent of angry words from spewing out of her mouth. "I don't think it's your right to question what any woman does in her personal life. Or to tell me that since I wrote an article defending a friend that I'm going to be an irresponsible doctor or I'm not going to do anything but sit at home all day and watch my kids." Once the words started coming out, she couldn't stop them.

"You claim to be so tolerant, but do you know how judgmental you sound right now? Telling me that I'm going to risk a patient's life for a ballet recital?" She glared at the black-haired girl, who at least had the decency to lower her gaze.

"And you." Kennedy turned to Marty. "When did a progressive editor's job become censoring anyone who didn't agree with your viewpoint? You guys called me in so you could hear what I had to say about my article. I told you. I wrote it because in last week's op-ed, you ripped into my friend. You've never met Sandy Lindgren. You have no idea what kind of woman she is. All you know is that she doesn't work a traditional job, and so you jump to the conclusion that she's some backwards, low-life ditz who's incapable of anything but baking and changing diapers. Do you know how ignorant that makes you all sound?

"You know I'm a Christian, you assume I'm conservative, so you jump to all kinds of conclusions about me. Know what? Christian women work all kinds of jobs. Some in the home, some out. And you know what else? They do that because it's their choice. Isn't that what you stand for? Freedom to choose the life you want to lead?"

"Not if your choices squash the freedom of others." Marty crossed her arms.

"Who's talking about squashing? When did I say anything about squashing? Take Sandy. How in the world can you look at all she does and tell me that she's kept other women from living their lives to the fullest?"

"Well, we all know that her husband's church …"

"I didn't ask about her husband's church," Kennedy interrupted. "I asked about Sandy herself. How does the fact that she stays at home and takes care of her son and grandkids hurt the other women who know her? What's so wrong with that lifestyle if it's truly her choice to make?"

Marty glanced around at the other editors. "Well, for one thing …" She hit her pen against the edge of the table a few times. "Her example itself is sending the wrong message. It's telling other females that if they don't stay home like she does, they're doing it wrong."

Kennedy shook her head. "Sandy would never say those things."

Marty shrugged. "I don't know that. All I know is her husband's the one spearheading this conference where a bunch of men are going to get together and talk about how to *keep their women in line* and anti-progressive garbage like that. And so even if your friend isn't actively contributing to that sort of chauvinistic mentality, she's definitely complicit."

Kennedy's heart was racing. Her hands were no longer clammy now but cold. Her jaw ached from being clenched so hard.

Apparently eager to make sure her words were the last, Marty composed herself and addressed the staff. "All right, so now we've heard all sides of the argument. What I'd like to do is have O'Brien and his writer friend step out, and we'll take our vote."

O'Brien stood to his feet. Kennedy did the same.

"Vote?" she asked. "What vote?"

She thought she detected a slight gleam in Marty's eyes. "The vote where we decide how to undo all the damage your little misogynistic column has caused."

CHAPTER 16

Kennedy followed O'Brien to a couch just outside the boardroom. "So now we wait?" she asked.

He nodded. "Now we wait."

She wanted to tell him something. Thank him maybe for the way he'd stood up for her, but she wasn't sure how to word it. She'd never really considered herself that articulate of an individual. She got good grades on her papers for her literature classes, but most of that had to do with knowing what kind of style and wording her professors expected from her. She'd never done anything like write a column for the paper before, and after today she was certain she wouldn't repeat the same mistake and try it again.

She glanced at the time and wondered if she should call Willow. Ask if there was any news about Carl. But of course, she didn't have her phone with her and didn't have a single number in her contacts list memorized. If God had made anything good come out of her interrogation meeting with the Voice editors, it was that it had taken her mind off Carl and his injuries. Even so, now she felt guilty that she'd wasted all her energy yelling at the editor-in-chief when she could have been praying for Carl's recovery.

Kennedy couldn't remember the last time she'd spilled her frustrations like that, at least not with someone other than her mom or dad. Guilt heated her core. She thought about Sandy, whom she'd been trying so hard to defend. She was so patient and gentle. In fact, today in the car was the first time Kennedy had heard Sandy actually snap at Woong, and that was only because he'd been disrespectful to the Lord.

Maybe there was a time and place for righteous anger, but Kennedy couldn't shake the feeling that all she'd done was let her temper take over and wasted her words on people who didn't want to hear what she had to say anyway. What was that verse in the Bible about casting your pearls before swine? She glanced at O'Brien, who was sulking next to her.

"It was nice of you to take my side in there," she said softly.

O'Brien looked up, as if he were surprised that she'd spoken. "Point taken, but for the record I'm not on your side. I'm on the side of open debate, and that's all."

Kennedy didn't know what to say. It was understandable if he was mad at her. She was the reason he was in trouble with his friends.

They were silent for several minutes. Through the drawn curtain in the meeting room, Kennedy could make out Marty's silhouette as she stood facing the other editors.

"Any guess how long this will take?" she finally worked up the courage to ask. Apparently, her little tantrum in the meeting room had used up her assertiveness quota for the day. Maybe more like the semester.

O'Brien shrugged. "What, this monkey trial? My guess is we'll get our answer in just another minute or two."

"So what exactly is it that they're voting on?"

He shrugged again. "Your article has already been printed. There's nothing they can do about that. It's just damage control now. Retractions, junk like that. And they're probably voting to see if I should keep my position on the paper or not."

"I'm really sorry you got involved in all this." What more could she say?

He let out his breath. "Oh, don't worry about that. If it wasn't your article, it would've been someone else's. It's ironic. They call my pages the forum section, but by definition the word *forum* means open debate. The free spread of ideas. If I had known when I signed up that all they wanted me to do was parrot back their orthodox party line, I would've never bothered. Or at least I would've had them change the name from *forum* to *propaganda*. It's much more fitting." He let out a mirthless chuckle. "And you … you sure played your cards right in there. Even before you walked into that room, they all had you pegged as some little dormouse who wouldn't dare have the guts to stand up for herself. I'm glad you proved them wrong." There was genuine respect in his eyes.

Kennedy returned his smile. "To be honest, that's not what I'm usually like, but they kept putting words in my mouth, twisting what I said."

"Yeah. It's what they do best. That and silence anyone who disagrees with them."

Kennedy rubbed her palm on the top of her pants, trying to figure out the best way to word her question. "Can I ask you something?"

"Sure." Another shrug. "What have we got to lose?"

She ignored his cynicism. "I got the feeling in there that you don't agree with what I had to say in my column," she began.

"Correct." He still didn't meet her eyes.

She licked her lips and continued. "But you defended me in the meeting room."

"Also correct. And you already hit on the difference. I don't agree with your statements. I think a woman is completely free to work whatever job she chooses."

Kennedy didn't bother to point out that she'd said almost the same thing verbatim in the meeting room but let O'Brien continue.

"So no, I don't personally support your opinions, but I support you as a freethinking student who has the right to hold whatever ideas you want to have. That's why I thought the forum section would be such a good fit for me. I see no reason to read only things that support what I already believe. When I pick up a book, for example, I'm not looking for something that's going to spoon-feed me what I already know. When I read something by an author whose opinions on the subject are exactly the same as my own, what do I gain other than a sense of self-righteousness? My idea for the forum section was to make it truly that — a forum where people with different viewpoints could have engaging, lively debates. Respectful debates of course. There's no reason for an ideological argument to be the foundation for a personal attack, which is exactly what happened to you in that meeting room. You asked why I defended you even though I don't believe in your viewpoint. and that's because you're obviously an intelligent individual, and sometimes what we all need is to be stared in the face by an argument that frightens us. That challenges our rigid and oh-so-precious convictions. You've got a right to be heard just as much as anyone else. And if people find your argument offensive, it's their job to prove you wrong rhetorically, not with personal jabs."

Kennedy hadn't expected such a long answer. She thought about Carl and Nick, about their frequent spats. As heated as their arguments got, at least they never resorted to those kind of base attacks. Speaking of attacks …

She looked at the time. If Willow hadn't already heard from Sandy by now, she probably wouldn't until morning. Kennedy couldn't picture Sandy sending out prayer chain updates this late at night no matter how serious things got. She glanced again at the drawn curtains of the Voice meeting room.

"You worried about the vote?" O'Brien asked. "No need to be. Since you're not on staff, the worst they can do is ban you from writing for us again."

"It's not that." Kennedy sighed. She really didn't want to go into details about what had happened to Carl, but it was all she was able to think about now and she found herself spelling out the abridged version of his injuries.

"That's messed up," was O'Brien's final assessment.

"Yeah." Kennedy couldn't have said it any better.

"So it was definitely intentional? It wasn't just like some bad accident or anything?"

Kennedy shook her head. "The police are already

involved, and we found the bookend the attacker used to knock him out with."

"That's messed up," he repeated.

"Yeah." She wondered if they were doomed to repeat the same two lines indefinitely like characters in a sci-fi book trapped in some sort of time loop.

"Think it has something to do with the that men's conference?"

O'Brien's question surprised her. She was in no mood to play detective. That was Drisklay's job.

"I don't know. I know people are upset about it, but I can't see anybody attacking him like that over it."

For a minute, Kennedy wondered if O'Brien was going to tell her how messed up it all was, but he simply shook his head.

"Wonder what they're taking so long for," he said a few minutes later. "Seems like it should be a pretty open and shut case."

"What do you think's going to happen to you?"

A shrug. "They'll probably vote me off the board."

She couldn't understand how he could sound so casual about it. "I'm really sorry. If I had known …"

"Don't worry about it," he interrupted. "I knew what I was doing, and I don't regret it. Even if they don't vote me off, I'll probably resign anyway. I've got a few friends who are thinking about working together to start a new paper. One that really does give free voice to the wide range of student opinions represented on campus." He gave her a soft smile. "You'd be welcome to write for us if you ever wanted."

She didn't have the heart to turn him down directly. "I'll keep that in mind."

The door to the conference room opened. Marty leaned out. "You can come in now. We're all finished."

CHAPTER 17

Kennedy sat down in the same chair she'd been in just a little while earlier. O'Brien remained standing.

"All right." Marty didn't look at either of them. "So, here's what's going to happen. O'Brien, you're off the staff. Although I enjoyed working with you and you had a lot of strong articles come out during your time here, tonight made it pretty clear that the Voice isn't a good fit for you."

"I couldn't agree with you more." O'Brien shot her an icy smile. None of the other editors would look him in the face.

Marty turned to Kennedy. "As for you, we expect a rebuttal in our hands by Monday afternoon at the latest. We all agree that the opinions you stated in your original column are problematic and potentially triggering to students who are experiencing gender-identity issues or self-directed misogyny, and that's just not something we can leave unadressed."

Kennedy glanced around the table. "You want me to take back what I already said?"

"That's the basic idea behind a rebuttal, correct?" Marty grinned sarcastically.

"But I already told you what I believe."

"Yeah, but unfortunately that's not the kind of archaic thinking that we at the Voice are able to condone. So what we'll need from you is two or three hundred words. Nothing lengthy."

Kennedy felt like she had as a third-grader being told she had to clean her room. "What happens if I don't submit a rebuttal?"

"Oh, I'm sure any of us here would be happy to write it for you. All you'd need to do is make any last-minute changes in style and voice."

"No, I mean what if I still stand by what I originally said?" Out of the corner of her eye, Kennedy caught O'Brien's wide grin.

Marty stared. "Excuse me?"

"I said I stand by what I wrote in my original article. I don't want to change anything."

Marty cleared her throat. "In that case …" She glanced around the table. "Well, in that case …"

"In that case," O'Brien broke in for her, "Kennedy,

you're free to go. And since I'm on my way out, too, I don't think anyone will mind if I congratulate you for writing the first original thought this paper has published in years."

O'Brien opened the door to the meeting room, and he and Kennedy exited the Voice office.

CHAPTER 18

O'Brien's dorm was in the opposite direction, so Kennedy wished him good night, thanked him again for his support, and hurried back toward her room. Her limbs were exhausted, her mind heavy. She wanted to sleep but knew it would still be a while before her thoughts would quiet down enough for her to get any rest.

The door to her room was slightly open when she got there. Willow's laughter rang through the hallway. Kennedy wondered if Nick had stopped by for another visit. As much fun as it usually was watching him and Willow interact with each other, she hadn't mentally prepared herself for a guest.

Especially not a guest who was four and a half feet tall.

"Hey, Kennedy!" Woong smiled broadly at her.

"What's going on?" she asked before she could remember any sort of decent etiquette.

"Woong was going to spend the night with his friends, the Linklaters," Willow explained in a voice that was a little louder and slower than necessary, "but then he thought to himself, *Hey, I bet my good friends Kennedy and Willow are having more fun than I am* so he asked to come over here."

Kennedy couldn't understand why her roommate was tilting her head toward Woong and apparently trying to send her some sort of telepathic message. All she could think to say was, "Why?"

"I got bored over there, so I asked Mrs. Linklater if I could call my mom. She's got to stay at the hospital with Dad, but she said she'd ask Nick if I could spend the night with him. Well, he was busy talking to some detective or other …"

Kennedy thought she saw Willow wince.

"So then my mom called you on account of you sometimes being my babysitter and stuff and nonsense like that, but instead of calling you, she called Willow, and then everything got a little confusing, and here I am."

Kennedy looked to her roommate for translation.

"I just got back from picking him up," Willow explained. "He was having a hard time sleeping." She lowered her voice. "Worried about his dad."

"Was not," Woong insisted with a pout.

Kennedy glanced around the room. "So what happens now? Is he sleeping here?"

"I wasn't sure," Willow told her. "I mean, I think Sandy was picturing you spending the night at their place, but she knew it was a lot to ask, and I wasn't sure how late your meeting would go, so I told her I'd pick up Woong, and then we'd decide what to do."

Woong adjusted himself in Willow's beanbag chair. "Well I figure that maybe I'll just sleep right here."

A college dorm was certainly no place for a little boy to spend the night, but Kennedy wondered what other options there were.

Willow leaned toward her desk mirror and applied some of her goat milk chap stick. "If Nick gets done talking with that Broccoli guy or whoever that detective is, he said he could stop by and take Woong to his place. I think that's plan A, but like I said, we don't know how long he's going to be."

"Why is the detective talking to him this late at night?" Kennedy asked, trying to gauge from Willow's expression how worried she was for her boyfriend.

"Beats me. This has all been by text. I haven't talked to him since he dropped us off earlier."

"Ok." Kennedy looked around the room again as if a third bed and a Woong-sized pair of pajamas might miraculously materialize. She wished she had a little privacy to talk with Willow about everything. Get the full account of Carl's health without having to worry about scaring Woong. Talk about that ridiculous meeting she'd just gotten out of.

Willow had taken one of her Alaska-themed quilts off her bed and threw it on top of Woong. "So you know it's really late, right? And you're probably going to have a busy day tomorrow, so I want you to try to get some sleep."

"What if I fall asleep and then Nick comes to take me to his apartment?"

"I'll tell him to carry you real quiet. Maybe you won't even wake up."

"I bet I will. I always do."

"Ok." Willow leaned over and adjusted the blanket around him. "For now, you just rest, all right? Do you need anything else before bed? Use the bathroom? Anything like that?"

Woong frowned. "My mom usually reads me some."

Kennedy was about to tell Woong that he'd have to sleep tonight without a story, but Willow was already over by Kennedy's desk. "What have you got that's good for a kid?" She ran her finger over a few of the titles.

"Nothing dystopian," Kennedy answered quickly. She thought about her American literature class. "What about *Little Women*?"

"Women?" Woong repeated. "Bleh. Why would I want to read a book about a bunch of girls?"

"There's lots of good books about girls," Willow told him. "Have you ever read *Anne of Green Gables*?"

"Yeah, my teacher read it to us in school last year. I liked the movie better. Especially the part where the old man grabs his arm, and then all of a sudden he's dead, and everyone's sad."

Willow glanced at Kennedy, trying to hide her smile.

"*Little Women*'s a good one," Kennedy interjected. "It's got these four sisters, and at the start of the book, it's the middle of the Civil War."

"Do any of them dress up like boys and run off to battle?" he asked.

"Well, no, but …"

"Do the soldiers come to their house, and the girls have to chase them off with guns and knives?"

"Not exactly."

"So what's it about then?" he demanded with a dubious pout.

"*Little Women* is a story about four sisters, and they … they …" Kennedy stopped. They what? Grow up and find husbands?

"They have lots of fun playing make-believe and putting

on plays and writing stories." Willow took the book off Kennedy's shelf. "It's really good. I think you'll like it."

"I don't know." Woong frowned at the cover picture of the four girls in their old-fashioned dresses.

"Why don't you let me read you the first chapter, and then you can let me know what you think?" Willow asked.

"It'll probably put me to sleep," Woong complained.

"That's the general idea," mumbled Willow, but Kennedy doubted he heard.

While Willow started to read, Kennedy got together the things she'd need for a shower. She didn't even have the energy to open her lab book and see which assignments from her students she still had to grade. One day at a time. She could worry about all that other stuff in the morning.

Shortly after moving into her dorm room at the start of the semester, Kennedy had found that the two small wardrobe-style closets could open up and make a perfect changing area that gave her just the amount of privacy she needed. She wrapped up in her bathrobe and grabbed her towel. Willow was at the part where Beth was trying to cheer her sisters up at the prospect of a Christmas with no presents as Kennedy slipped on her waterproof flip-flops, headed into the hallway, and nearly bumped into someone coming around the corner. "I'm sorry," she mumbled without raising her eyes.

"No worries. Where you off to so late?"

She glanced up when she recognized the voice. "Oh, hey, Nick. I didn't realize it was you."

He smiled. "Yeah. I noticed. What's going on?"

She clutched her toiletry caddy against herself and felt her cheeks grow hot. Her long-sleeved bathrobe covered everything but her flip-flops, but she still felt exposed. "I was on my way to take a shower. Willow's in there reading to Woong." She hoped Nick would take the hint and go in, but he just smiled.

"Yeah, I had a lot of different texts from Willow and Sandy, and I couldn't keep everything straight. I thought he'd be here though. I guess I'm supposed to take him home with me, right? It's been such a crazy night. I just finished meeting with that detective."

"Oh." Kennedy reminded herself that her typical jeans and sweaters were far more form-fitting and revealing than an oversized fluffy bathrobe. She was an adult and quite capable of having a conversation like this even if she wasn't as appropriately attired as she'd like to be. "Did it go all right?"

He nodded. "Yeah. Another hour answering the same questions he asked me this afternoon. You know how it is. Wants me to come up with a list of people who might have had it in for Pastor Carl."

Kennedy still had a hard time accepting that what happened to Carl was real and not some sort of bad hallucination or daydream. "Who would want to hurt him?"

Nick shrugged. "Unfortunately, there's a lot of people fitting that description. That's what I told the detective."

Kennedy still couldn't wrap her mind around it. "Like who?"

"Like Sandra Green, the head of that feminist movement. She's not the biggest fan of Truth Warriors, and I can't say that I blame her."

Kennedy wasn't ready to listen to a political tirade, but she found herself asking all the same, "What's wrong with Truth Warriors?"

"Do you know much about the conferences?" Nick asked.

"No. Just that they're for men, to encourage them to grow in their walk with God, that sort of thing."

"Well, the *encouragement* they receive is questionable to say the least. Those men who signed up for Carl's Truth Warriors conference, they're going to be *encouraged* to lead their wives, and of course all the speakers are going to stand up there and talk about how that leadership needs to be covered in a spirit of gentleness and love. But seriously, how many men are going to listen to that part, and how many are just going to go home and demand blind submission from their spouses? And what about all the male-female relationships that aren't marriages? Hmm? What then? And where does it end? If men are supposed to be the leaders of the home, what does that mean for the mother of teenage boys? What's going to happen to Mr. Joe Christian who goes to Truth Warriors and then decides his privilege as a male, as the God-ordained leader of the world, means that he doesn't have to listen to his female boss?"

Kennedy wasn't ready for this kind of discussion. All she wanted was a shower.

Nick looked at the ground. "Sorry. This has been on my mind a lot. I don't even remember how we got on it."

"You were just talking about Carl and the detective."

He nodded. "Yeah. And you know how much I love Carl. I really do, but he's got these blind sides. He doesn't see the injustices he's perpetuating. So St. Margaret's has no women pastors, right? Because we all know what the Bible has to say about that." He rolled his eyes. "But we can hire a *women's ministry leader*. And what's she do? She pastors the women of the church. She does every single thing Carl and I do, but she's not a pastor. She's not allowed to be part of the elder board. Even though Carl obviously thinks highly enough of her to entrust the spiritual well-being of half his adult congregation to her leadership. And do you think she makes close to the same amount of money as Carl does? Not a chance.

"And don't even get me started on poor Dawn. That woman has been Carl's secretary since the day he started St. Margaret's Church. Any guess what her salary is? Come on. Take a stab at it."

Kennedy didn't know enough about American economics to even have a bad estimate to offer. "Minimum wage?"

He laughed. "She'd be lucky if it were that much. Nope. She gets a monthly stipend of four hundred dollars a month. Four hundred dollars a month, and she's in that office at least thirty hours a week."

This was the first Kennedy had heard about Dawn getting paid at all. "I had the feeling she was a volunteer there."

"She basically is. Which is what I'm saying. You think they'd dare treat a man that way?"

Kennedy didn't know how to answer. "Why doesn't she ask for more money then?"

"Oh, it's not about the money." He waved his hand in the air dismissively. "Her husband's got this crazy Wall Street-type job. She doesn't have to work at all, but she wants to serve the church."

Kennedy didn't see what the problem was then, but Nick kept railing against the injustices inherent in the St. Margaret pay scale.

"It's not the fact that she's not getting paid what she's worth. It's the fact that the elders just assume that since her husband's going to take care of all the bills, they can count on Dawn basically for slave labor."

"She seems content whenever I go in," Kennedy remarked, trying to gauge if she knew the secretary enough to jump to any sort of conclusion.

Nick shrugged. "Yeah, she probably doesn't even know how poorly she's being treated." He shuffled his weight from one foot to the other. "Hey, mind if I ask you a question? It's a little awkward."

Kennedy stared down at her front before she realized the awkwardness had to do with his question and not her appearance. "Sure. Go ahead." Why couldn't he have come just a minute later? Two students walked by, apparently oblivious to the fact that one of their dormmates was having a conversation in the middle of the hallway wearing nothing but her bathrobe.

Nick cleared his throat. "So, I was wondering about Willow, and well, it was really strange having that detective single me out, you know. Because of my fight with Carl earlier.

And well, I mean, I know we all know I didn't have anything to do with it, but what's been eating at me all night … I tried calling Willow several times, and when we grabbed dinner, she seemed a little off, and she hasn't said all that much to me today, and I guess what I'm wondering is if she's said anything to you … about that sort of stuff, you know, like me and the detective and what happened earlier."

It wasn't until she caught him staring at her so expectantly that Kennedy realized he was waiting for a response. "So you want to know …" she began, hoping her brain would fill in the pieces she must have missed. Had that rambling run-on sentence contained an actual question?

"Does she think I'm guilty?"

Kennedy nearly laughed but stopped herself when she saw how earnest he looked. "No, of course not." She was surprised that his features still didn't change. "No," she repeated more adamantly. "Nobody really believes that. Even the detective. He's just got to follow up on everything. You know how it is."

Nick fingered one of his dreadlocks. "You sure? She's not even a tiny bit suspicious?"

Kennedy wanted to tell Nick that nobody who knew him could believe he'd have the intestinal fortitude to attack someone as formidable as Carl, but she could tell he needed more assurance than that. "It's ok." She gave him a smile, forgetting for the moment about her silly bathrobe. "Willow adores you more than anything. You could be a serial killer, and she'd be the last person in the world to harbor a single suspicion."

Nick winced.

She cleared her throat. "So, did you find anything out about Carl? I've been tied up all night. I haven't been able to check my phone or even get Willow to fill me in yet. Is there any news?"

Nick was staring over her shoulder. "Not that I've heard. The detective isn't exactly Mr. Chatty if you know what I mean."

"Yeah." Kennedy rolled her eyes. "You've got that right."

"So you're sure …" Nick began and then stopped himself. "You're sure Willow's ok? With me, I mean?"

"Of course. Go on in there. I'll probably see you in a few minutes, or else have a good night."

"Ok." He took a step past her then stopped. "Hey, Kennedy?"

"What?" She turned around.

He offered a shy smile. "Thanks for talking things through with me. I really appreciate that."

"No problem. We all know you're perfectly innocent."

Nick grimaced and then turned around. Kennedy made her way to the showers, puzzling the entire time over his expression and wondering if she'd said something wrong.

CHAPTER 19

Fifteen minutes later, showered and a little more relaxed than she'd been after her meeting with the Voice staff, Kennedy made her way back to her room. She could hear Willow and Nick fighting from the opposite side of the hallway. Of course, some of that had to do with her roommate's frustrating habit of never shutting the door entirely, but she couldn't remember the two of them getting so heated in the past.

"Who do you think you are, blaming him for what happened?" Willow shouted.

They both fell silent when Kennedy entered the room. The heat from their argument hung heavy in the air like smog. Neither one acknowledged Kennedy as she made her way to her bedside and began putting away her toiletries.

"I'm not saying he deserved it." Nick's voice was softer when he finally spoke up, but Kennedy could tell from his shaky tone he was working hard to mask his rage. "All I'm saying is that with his old-fashioned views on everything and then this whole mess he got the church into planning the Truth Warriors conference, it's not surprising to me that someone got worked up enough to attack him."

Kennedy debated if she wanted to waste the time and energy to dry her hair. It would drown out a little bit of Willow and Nick's spat, which would be nice, but her entire body longed to sink down into her bed and forget everything that had happened over the past twenty-four hours.

"That's fabulous coming from you," Willow retorted. "The one who's always standing up for the little man, the one with all your progressive philosophy. I suppose victim blaming is fair game now as long as the victim's views don't agree with your own?"

Nick began pacing. "I wasn't victim blaming."

Kennedy plugged in her hairdryer but still couldn't decide if she should use it. Woong was asleep in the purple beanbag chair, and Kennedy hated the thought of waking him up. Then again, if he could sleep through an argument like this, he could probably sleep through the tribulation.

"You know what I don't get?" Willow asked. "I don't get how somebody who's as concerned about issues of social justice as you can be so calloused toward your friend. What if this was some random pastor you read about in the news? What if you had no idea what his political views were or what presidential candidate he voted for? I've seen you cry before, remember that? I've seen you watch a documentary about the way those school kids were being treated in Detroit with all those toxins in their playground and poison in the water, and you sobbed your heart out."

"I was just …" Nick began, but Willow cut him off.

"I'm not mentioning that to make you feel bad. In fact, that night I came back and told Kennedy I'd found the man I wanted to spend the rest of my life with. Don't look at me like that. Ask her yourself if you don't believe me."

Kennedy was still staring at the hairdryer in her hand, still trying to decide if falling asleep now would be worth the bed head she'd wake up with in the morning.

"You are the most socially responsible, compassionate man I've ever met," Willow continued. "But you're as stubborn as a mule. And a smelly, ugly mule at that. You and Carl have this twisted, quasi-sadistic love-to-hate-him kind of relationship that I don't even pretend to understand, but beneath all those superficial disagreements, the two of you have always come together in the end and reaffirmed your love for each other. And now he's hurt, and maybe even dying for all we know, and when I would expect you to be the most compassionate, the most concerned, you're sitting here rattling off all the reasons why Carl brought it on himself."

Willow yanked her brush through her hair. “And I’m sitting here listening to you berate your friend, and all I’m left to wonder now is what happened to that man I fell in love with, the man who cried during a documentary about kids he’s never met in Detroit but apparently doesn’t have a single tear to shed for his pastor and mentor who at this moment is on a ventilator struggling to survive.”

Kennedy put her hairdryer away, wondering how inconspicuously she could tuck herself into bed and try to shut out Willow’s words.

Nick stopped his pacing and sat down beside Willow on her mattress. “I suppose you’re right. I was acting like a jerk.”

Willow rubbed his back. “Yeah, but you’re the jerk I love.”

Nick stared at his hands and let out a sigh. “It’s just that …” His dreadlocks fell toward the floor, and he shook his head. “It’s just that it’s easier to be angry. Know what I mean?”

“No,” Willow answered. “What do you mean?”

It took Nick several seconds to respond. “I mean that it’s easier to pretend I’m still mad at him. Easier to pretend like this is his fault. Because otherwise all I can do is blame myself. I was there just a few minutes before it happened.

Maybe I could have stopped it. Or maybe I'd made Carl so upset with all the debating that he couldn't see who was coming. Couldn't fight them off. That's what I mean when I say it's easier to be angry. You tell me that I've lost my sense of compassion, that I'm as stubborn as a … well, we all heard what you had to say about that." He smiled faintly and gently nudged Willow's side.

"Yeah, I'll admit it wasn't one of my finer moments."

Nick shrugged. "No, but it wasn't that far from the truth. It's just so hard for me to accept that any of this is really happening. That Carl … that he's …" Nick's voice broke, and he buried his face in his hands while Willow murmured reassurances into his ear.

Kennedy plugged in her hairdryer for a second time and let the loud noise drown out Nick's cries.

CHAPTER 20

Blinding sunlight streamed in from the window. Kennedy rolled over. What time was it? She squinted at her phone. Ten after nine? She couldn't remember the last time she'd slept in so late. In fact, she didn't even remember falling asleep. She knew something had happened last night. What was it?

"No, I'm sorry. She's not up yet." Was that Willow talking? Why was she whispering?

"We had a meeting scheduled for this morning."

Kennedy recognized the voice but couldn't place it, not until her brain had a little more chance to wake up.

"She didn't say anything about it to me," her roommate snapped.

"Does she tell you everything?"

Kennedy sat up in bed. "Who's there?" she asked in a groggy voice.

Willow stepped aside to reveal Ian, the red-haired journalist. Kennedy had talked to him yesterday when she was at the hospital. The hospital … Memories from Carl's attack crashed and swirled in her mind.

"Good morning." He offered a small smile. "Sorry if I woke you up. I tried texting you to see if we were still on for breakfast, but I never got a reply."

At the word *breakfast*, Willow's entire countenance changed. She let out an airy laugh. "Something you learn about Kennedy real quick is that she's got a moral compulsion against checking her messages or keeping her phone charged. Just one of those little idiosyncrasies you grow to love about her."

Willow flung open Kennedy's small wardrobe, pulled out a pair of jeans and a new blouse they'd bought on an impromptu shopping spree together and tossed them onto Kennedy's bed. "You get up and get ready, sunshine," Willow told her then turned to Ian. "And you wait outside until she's presentable. Don't worry, I won't make you wait too long."

She closed the door in Ian's face and ran to Kennedy. "You didn't tell me you had a date with the ginger."

"It's not a date." Kennedy's temples were throbbing. She wasn't a regular caffeine drinker, but she'd need more than a few sips of coffee this morning to get her brain as alert as it needed to be. What day was it, anyway? She had lit class in a few hours and then lab, right? Wait, lab?

She sat up in bed. "I can't go out. I have all my students' reports to grade."

Willow pulled down Kennedy's blankets. "Of course you have time for breakfast. Especially with that cute journalist. Maybe I shouldn't be saying this, but I've been praying that God would send you somebody after Dominic … well, you know. And I've only been at this praying thing for a little while, so think what it's doing to my brand-new faith to see you finally starting to date again. So you can't let me down now. And someone like the journalist. Didn't I tell you the very first time I saw him that he's absolutely scrumptious? I mean, Dominic wasn't bad looking if you're into the whole huggable-teddy-bear-with-a-beard sort of feel. But the ginger … when did you even start talking to him anyway? Last I heard, wasn't he filming in your parents' neck of the woods in China or something?"

Kennedy was behind her closet door and halfway dressed, but even though her body was out of bed, her brain couldn't keep up with all of Willow's questions.

"So where you going?" Willow asked. "Is he taking you someplace fancy?" She let out a sigh. "First dates are so romantic. It's too bad Nick and I will never have another."

"It's not a date." Kennedy emerged from the makeshift dressing room.

Willow rolled her eyes. "Sure it isn't. And I'm a virgin. I mean, ok, so maybe it's a bad example since I'm doing the whole abstinence thing now, but you get my point."

Still droopy with exhaustion and trying to recall if she had officially agreed on a time to meet Ian this morning, Kennedy grabbed a pair of socks from her dresser drawer.

"No," Willow protested. "Look outside. It's a gorgeous sunny day. And what about that cute pedicure I gave you? You can't hide those toes in your old worn-out tennies." She reached under her own bed. "Here, wear my platforms. They'll go perfect with those jeans." After tossing the sandals onto the floor by Kennedy's bare feet, Willow rummaged through her desk. "Want to borrow some earrings? I have these beaded ones you like, but I think the turquoise look more mature. Which is what you're going for, because this ginger, how old is he again?"

Kennedy didn't have time to answer before Willow started brushing her hair for her. "If he weren't waiting right out there, I'd mousse it up for you. But this will have to do." She stepped back and crossed her arms. "There you go. Perfect for a breakfast out." Another loud sigh. "Morning dates are so dreamy."

"It's not a date," Kennedy repeated right before Willow shoved her out their bedroom door.

CHAPTER 21

"Sorry again for waking you up." Ian let out a chuckle as he and Kennedy walked across campus.

"That's all right," Kennedy assured him while simultaneously imagining how she'd get back at Willow for making such a big deal about a simple breakfast out.

They walked in silence for a while. Kennedy wondered what Ian was thinking about. She'd run into him randomly several times so far during her time as an undergrad at Harvard, but they'd never gotten the chance to say more than a few words to each other in any given instance.

Once off-campus, they waited until it was safe to cross the street into Harvard Square. Ian suggested they walk over to L'Aroma Bakery. The thought of a buttery crusted quiche made Kennedy's mouth water so much that she probably couldn't have protested without drooling even if she had reason to. At least by going to L'Aroma, she could eat a quick breakfast and arrive back at her dorm in less than an hour. Plenty of time to finish grading all those lab reports.

At least she hoped so, seeing as how she still couldn't remember how many more there were left. She struggled to match Ian's pace while keeping her balance in Willow's platform sandals. Once they made it to the other side of the street, he slowed down and gave her a gentle smile. "Guess it's been a rough week for you, hasn't it?"

Maybe it was because he was a member of the press or maybe because Kennedy didn't know him all that well, but she still wasn't sure how much she should trust someone like Ian. On the one hand, he'd helped out in the past when she'd found herself in difficult situations, but there was so much she didn't know about him. And yet, it always seemed as if he knew everything about her.

"Yeah," she agreed, "I can definitely say I've had easier weeks this semester." She realized she hadn't asked Willow for any updates on Carl's condition. She also realized she'd left her phone back in her room.

"You're a junior now, right?" Ian asked.

"Right."

"Still premed?"

"Yeah." Kennedy already regretted letting her roommate talk her into this. Now that the fresh air and sunshine had revived her, she was able to remember the details of Ian's phone call yesterday and knew with almost a hundred percent certainty that even though he'd mentioned breakfast, they'd never actually made any sort of formal agreement.

Thankfully, L'Aroma Bakery was only a few minutes' walk away. It was crowded as usual, but they found a table in the corner that offered some privacy.

"Order anything you'd like," Ian told her. "Or we can split something. My treat." He smiled at her, and Kennedy noticed a dimple right in the middle of his chin. She tried not to blush when she recalled what a big deal Willow had made about their time out together. If it hadn't been for that, Kennedy could treat this interview just like anything else, something to check off her to-do list before she moved on to her next assignment. But now that Willow had filled her head with all her dramatic sighs and reminiscences about the magic of first dates and romantic breakfasts, Kennedy was jittery even before the waitress came and filled her mug with coffee.

This isn't a date, Kennedy reminded herself as Ian asked about her semester.

This isn't a date, she repeated when the waitress brought a platter full of fruit and a giant omelet, which Ian split before setting one half in front of her.

This isn't a date. She glanced at her nearly empty plate and realized she and Ian had been talking about their respective times in East Asia and at Harvard, but that he hadn't asked her a single question about her article by the time the server came back with the bill.

He reached into his pocket.

"You sure you don't want me to pitch in?" Kennedy asked.

He smiled, revealing that boyish dimple. How had she not noticed it before? "No, thank you. It's one of the perks of being freelance." He pulled out his credit card and set it on top of the receipt.

Kennedy gave him a quizzical look.

"Tax write-off," he explained and then frowned. "Oh, that sounded bad. I'm sorry."

She smiled reassuringly. "No, don't apologize or anything. It's just that when you called yesterday and said you wanted to talk, I was expecting it would be about the article."

"You're right. My bad. I just have a real hard time jumping straight into work, especially before I've had any caffeine." He finished off his second cup of coffee. "Tell you what. The weather is fantastic out there. Care to take a walk around Harvard Square?"

Kennedy wished Willow were here so she could kick her under the table with her stupid high-heeled sandals. She wiped her face with her napkin, still trying to figure out why she felt let-down after such a delicious breakfast and interesting conversation. As it turned out, Ian was as involved in the North Korean refugee crisis in China as her parents were, although in a far more public way. While her parents helped harbor refugees in secret, Ian documented the many human rights abuses on both sides of the Chinese-North Korean border. He traveled to the region nearly every year collecting interviews which would eventually be compiled into a full-length documentary. He'd even gone into North Korea twice to collect illegal footage for his project.

"My magnum opus," he'd called it. "At least my first," he added with a jocular twinkle in his green eyes.

They stepped outside into the fresh air. Fall was in no hurry this year. The leaves on the trees had just started to lose their first hint of chlorophyll, and if all she had to judge by was the chirping of the birds, Kennedy might have guessed it was the middle of May.

Ian's pace was slow, and she tried not to think about those lab reports she still needed to grade. She'd started them last weekend. She knew she'd gotten through at least the first four or five, hadn't she? What time was it, anyway? She hated not having her phone on her. What if Sandy was trying to call? What if there was more news about Carl?

She thought it was strange that the subject of her pastor's accident hadn't come up all morning. She didn't know if it was on the news at this point, but St. Margaret's was one of the largest churches in Cambridge and had already been in the limelight because of the upcoming Truth Warriors conference. The entire state of Massachusetts probably knew more about Carl's condition than she did.

"You ever been in that little coffee shop over there?" Ian pointed across the street.

"No. It looks nice." Had she ever noticed it before? She should come up with a way to tell him she had to get back to campus soon. All those lab reports …

"There's this coffee place in Tumen, not too far from where your parents live," Ian said. "Run by Canadian missionaries. Nicest people you'd ever meet." His voice trailed off.

Kennedy tried to think of a way to steer the conversation toward her massive to-do list for the day. When had she gotten this tongue-tied? She cleared her throat. "So, listen, about our interview …"

"Right." Ian's pace sped up the faster he talked. Another twenty minutes like this, and Kennedy's feet might never recover. He looked across the street one more time. "So, any chance you've got room for one more cup of coffee?"

Kennedy wished she could tell him she'd love to, but schoolwork had to come first. And Carl. How could she have gone all morning without trying to find out how he was? How calloused could she be? She took in a deep breath. "I'm sorry. It's been really fun, but I honestly wasn't expecting it to last this long. I've got class before long, and I still have a bunch of reports to grade."

"Really?" His eyes lit up. "Are you a TA? For what? No, you can tell me later. I'm sorry. I should have been paying more attention to the time. Do you really have to go back so soon? I was hoping to ask you a few questions …"

"I know." She hated feeling like she was letting him down. She glanced at the little beatnik coffee shop across the street. "Maybe we can get that coffee another morning?"

Ian smiled. "Deal. And in the meantime, you'll let me walk you back to campus and ask a few questions about your article on the way, right?"

"Sure."

They turned around when Ian's phone rang. "Oh, I better see who that is. Might be for work." He took his cell out of his pocket and squinted at the screen. "Are you calling me?" he asked.

"What?"

He showed her his phone. "This is your number. At least,

that's what caller ID says."

Kennedy shook her head. "I left my cell back at the dorm."

He answered his cell. They were almost back to L'Aroma Bakery where they'd spent their morning talking about nothing. About everything.

Ian frowned. He had such expressive features. "Kennedy? Yeah. She's here. Who's this?"

She didn't realize that Ian had stopped walking until she nearly bumped into him.

"Sure." His eyes softened. Was he worried? Sad? "Ok, here she is." He held out his phone. "It's your roommate. Something about your pastor."

Kennedy held her breath and had to remind herself that a simple piece of electronics couldn't physically hurt her. She took Ian's cell phone, placed it against her ear, and croaked, "Hello?"

Willow's voice on the other line was breathless. "Kennedy. Thank God I got hold of you. Do you know how many searches you get when you google *red-haired journalists in Cambridge*? It took me forever just to track down Ginger's name, and then I had to find him on your phone, and after that … oh, never mind. Sandy called. It's bad news."

Kennedy steadied herself against a newspaper stand. "How bad?"

"Really bad," Willow answered. "I mean, no, not *that* bad. I mean, he's not … you know, he isn't … He's still at the hospital. But they got him stable enough that the doctors wanted to do an MRI, you know, to assess how bad the damage was to his brain."

Kennedy wanted to propel herself through time and get to the part of the call when Willow actually told her what was wrong. "And?"

Willow sniffed. "I couldn't understand all the medical details. Sandy called because she thought maybe you could help explain it to her."

"Explain what?" Kennedy turned so she didn't have to look at Ian, but she could still feel the worry and compassion from his gaze. This wasn't his conversation. He didn't know Carl. Wasn't close to him like Kennedy was.

On the other line, Kennedy heard what sounded like paper rustling. What was Willow doing?

"Ok, here's what Sandy said. The MRI showed several different types of hemorrhaging, and then there was something about swelling, and the bottom line is she says the doctors aren't sure he's ever getting off that ventilator."

CHAPTER 22

Kennedy would have never guessed she could make it from L'Aroma Bakery to Willow's car in J Lot in just a little over five minutes. Shortly after wishing Ian her very hasty and probably not-so-polite goodbye, she'd taken off the platform sandals and ran the rest of the way barefoot, vowing to never let her roommate talk her out of her comfortable tennis shoes again.

Kennedy reached student parking as Willow headed over from the opposite direction.

"Dude." Willow looked Kennedy up and down. "You're a mess."

"I know." Kennedy threw open the passenger door to her roommate's car. "Let's go."

Willow sat down beside her and offered a sympathetic gaze.

Kennedy was in no mood for compassion right now. "What's happened to Carl?" She mentally calculated down to the minute when they could arrive at Providence Hospital and prayed that the rush-hour congestion would have died down by now.

"I've already told you what I know." Willow pulled out of the parking lot and merged into the oncoming traffic.

Kennedy wished Willow's car had a siren or something so they didn't have to crawl at this snail's pace. "So Sandy called?" She wanted Willow to start over from the beginning. She'd been so worried about getting herself to J Lot that she'd forgotten all the details Willow had told her previously, scant as they were.

"Yeah." Willow was almost shouting to be heard over the sounds of her engine and rock station. "She said they did an MRI this morning, and the damage is more extensive than they expected. Basically, she thinks that the only help for Carl now will be some kind of miracle. That's why she's called a few of us over to pray for him."

"So we'll be meeting others there?"

"Yeah. I don't know who, but I figured you wouldn't want to miss it."

Kennedy glanced at the time. There was no way she'd make it to her lit class, which wouldn't end her college career. She was so far ahead in her reading she could probably write the remainder of her papers and finish the course half a semester early if she really wanted. It wasn't like her to skip out on a class, but this was important. Willow was right. She wouldn't miss Carl's prayer meeting for anything.

But wait, didn't she have some other obligation today?

Oh, no.

"I can't go. I forgot all about my lab this afternoon." Why had she ever let Professor Adell talk her into becoming a TA?

Willow scrunched up her moussed hair. "Actually …"

Kennedy turned down the music. If her roommate wasn't using hearing aids by the time she was fifty, it would be a miracle in and of itself.

Willow cleared her throat. "Ok, so I didn't want to tell you this right away, but I guess it's best to come out now."

Kennedy didn't know what she was talking about. All she knew was those stupid lab reports were going to keep her from Carl's bedside to pray for him as he lay dying. Whatever Willow had to tell her, she was in no mood for a guessing game. "What is it?"

"Ok, well, you know how some kids on campus got upset about your article, right? Calling it misogynistic and all that junk."

"Yeah." What did any of this have to do with Carl or her lab class?

"So, I had your phone this morning because you forgot it when you and Ginger went out for your little date, which you know I'm dying to hear all about even though now's not the best time. Anyway, you left your phone in the bedroom, but surprise of surprises, it was actually charged. So someone called, and it was a local number without a name, so I thought it might be Sandy at the hospital, and I knew you would want to hear how Carl was doing right away, so I answered it. Only it wasn't her."

"Are you or aren't you going to turn around and take me back so I don't miss my lab?" Kennedy interrupted.

"That's the thing." Willow reached out like she was about to turn up the radio but stopped herself. "So, it wasn't Sandy on the phone. It was your chemistry professor, Adell. And she was all upset that she couldn't get hold of you and said it was *of tantamount importance,* and so to calm her down I told her I could give you a message. So that's what I'm doing. And I'm sorry because I know it's horrible timing with Carl being so bad off, and you having to cut your date with Ginger short, but maybe it's for the best. You know how you're always telling me God works all things together for good, right? Maybe this is one of those times. So don't freak out on me, and remember I'm just the messenger, ok?"

"What is it?" Kennedy didn't mean to snap, but she couldn't help it. "Just tell me," she added in a more conciliatory tone.

Willow took in a deep breath. "Ok, so Adell said there's a student or two in your lab that was offended by your article, and I guess they made a big enough stink about it that they went to Adell's supervisor — this is how she made it out to sound at least — and got the science department head to suspend your teaching privileges while they *look into the allegations* or whatever it is they've got to do. I have no idea if it's just to shut these students up or if they're really serious about getting you in trouble or what, but Adell called to tell you that as of right now, you're out of a teaching job."

"What?" Kennedy would be surprised if she didn't end up with whiplash the way she snapped her head around toward Willow.

"Hey, don't take it out on me. Remember, I'm just passing on the message. And Adell, she didn't come right out and say so, but I got the sense she disagreed with the department head. She told me to tell you she was sorry, at the very least."

"That's ridiculous." What in the world did Kennedy's view on motherhood have to do with her ability to teach chemistry? Besides, she'd never said in her article that all women should do nothing but raise babies and mop floors. She just wanted people to stop treating any stay-at-home mom — especially one as kind and capable as Sandy — like a sub-par human being, like a tragic case of someone who'd never realized her full potential, like a threat to the progressive women's movement.

"Try not to worry about it right now."

"Easy for you to say." Kennedy realized it was senseless to get angry at Willow, but all that pent-up stress needed some sort of an outlet. "And how am I supposed to do that? I defended a friend, and look what happened. I got the only editor who ever stood up for me fired, I got my dorm building vandalized, and now I've lost my job. So remind me again what's not to worry about?"

Willow didn't respond. Kennedy wouldn't blame her if she was mad now. That'd be the perfect way to top off an already horrible morning.

After a few minutes of silence, Willow turned up the radio station just a little. "I'm sorry," she said as the Providence parking structure loomed into view.

Kennedy was too ashamed of herself and her petty little outburst to respond.

CHAPTER 23

Once inside Providence, Kennedy followed Willow, wondering what to expect when she got up to Carl's floor. Last she heard, he was in the ICU. Would the hospital staff even let them in to visit?

On the way up in the elevator, Kennedy broke the strained silence. "I'm sorry I got so upset in the car. You know I wasn't mad at you, right?"

Willow rubbed her back. "Of course. Hey, I'm just glad to see you standing up for yourself every once in a while. It's been a long time coming."

Kennedy didn't reply. Willow's phone beeped, and she reached into her purse. "Oh, that's Nick." She stared at her screen. "I guess he can't make the prayer meeting. That's too bad."

"What's going on?" Kennedy asked, hoping it didn't have any more to do with Detective Drisklay or the investigation about Carl's assault.

Willow shrugged. "Didn't say. This has been really hard

on him, you know. He thinks of Carl like a dad."

Kennedy figured some adults had that sort of argumentative relationship with their fathers, but she didn't think it sounded all that pleasant. "You know what I've been wondering for a while now?"

Willow was digging around in her purse after she put her phone away. "Hmm?"

"How Carl and Nick managed to work together all these years in the first place. I mean, I guess it's one thing to have a friend who believes so differently from you, but if you're a pastor of a prominent church and you're known for being so conservative …" She wasn't quite sure how to complete her sentence.

"Then why do you put up with someone like Nick in the first place?" Willow finished for her.

Kennedy smiled. "Yeah."

The girls got out of the elevator and started the long walk down the hallway to the ICU. "It's pretty complicated," Willow began. "I'm surprised Sandy never told you the story."

"What story?"

"You know, why Carl's never fired Nick even with all their political disagreements. Why Nick adores Carl even if he'll hardly ever come right out and say so. Why he's so upset now with Carl being in such bad shape …" Her voice died down at the sight of over a dozen people standing around the nurses' station.

"What do you suppose that is?" Kennedy asked.

Willow fingered her long beaded earring. "My guess is that's Carl's prayer team."

No wonder the nurse looked panicked. As they got closer, Kennedy could hear her words. "I'm sorry. I can only let immediate family members in."

Sandy was there, standing behind someone who looked like he could be Carl's older, larger brother. She smoothed out her French braid. "All right, friends, we don't want to cause the staff here any problems. There's just too many of us, and Carl's condition is too uncertain right now. It wouldn't be right for us all to go in his room. But we came here to pray, and the charge nurse is graciously allowing us to meet down the hall in the little conference center. We can all pray for Carl there."

Sandy smiled when she came up to Kennedy and Willow. "Good morning, my girls. I'm so thankful you came." She gave them both hugs. "I wish we could go in and pray for Carl by his bedside, but it's just not going to work out today."

Kennedy gave her hand a squeeze. "That's ok. I think it's

great you put this all together."

"It was Woong's idea, actually," Sandy admitted.

"Really?"

"Yeah, he's been asking all kinds of questions about faith and prayer since he got so sick last spring. It's hard because I want him to remember that we can trust God for miracles, but I'm just not sure this time that the miracle's coming."

Willow rubbed Sandy on the back. "Don't talk like that. We all know God's going to pull Carl through this, and Woong's going to have an even stronger faith after his dad's healed."

Sandy smiled sadly but didn't reply.

Kennedy tried to redirect the subject. "Where is Woong, by the way?"

"He's reading a Bible joke book to his dad, the one Carl sometimes uses for opening up his sermons. He …" Sandy sniffed. "Well, he said he thought that's what his dad would like to hear."

"How sweet," Willow cooed.

Sandy looked like she was about to cry. To get her mind off her husband, Kennedy offered lamely, "A lot of people showed up today."

Another tired smile. "Sure did. That man is so well-loved and well-respected. It would be such a tragedy if … well, never mind me. I didn't sleep well last night, and that always turns me into a grouch."

Kennedy caught Willow's grin and had to smile herself. On a bad day, Sandy was still nicer than just about everyone else on the globe.

Once everyone was crowded around a meeting table designed for a group about half as large, Sandy called for everyone's attention. She had no problem taking charge in the cramped conference room.

"First of all, I can't tell you what a blessing and an honor it is to have all of you come out here to join me in prayer for my Carl. You know that man has touched so many lives, but he's so humble I don't think he realizes the half of it. The fact that all of you showed up here is a testimony to Carl's love for God and his love for others. I know all of us around this table have been touched by his faith and his teaching and his encouragement."

There were nods of general agreement all around, but nobody tried to interrupt Sandy's speech.

"Now, I know the prayer chain's been sending out updates, but I'm still getting lots of questions about what happened, so I figured that before we started to pray, I'd fill you in on everything I know so we're all on the same page. Yesterday afternoon, while he was in his office working,

Carl was hit on the head with a heavy bookend. Knocked him out. At first, we were only worried about the blood loss, but on the way to the hospital, he had an incident. They still don't know exactly what. Brain bleed maybe, head trauma, something like that. That's why he's on the ventilator now. Last night we were hopeful that once he got stable and they got the internal bleeding and swelling under control, he'd be just fine. He had a peaceful night. No major scares or anything, but when they turned down the machine to see how he'd do on his own, his brain still wasn't telling his body to breathe like it should. So they did an MRI, and I can't remember all the medical details, but the general impression I got from the meeting with the neurologist is that the injuries Carl sustained, both the initial hit to the head and all the internal wounds that followed, are far more serious than anyone expected."

She paused. Kennedy didn't know if she was done or if there was more to it. Sandy was always so positive, so encouraging. Kennedy felt like everyone around the room was waiting for some word of hope or comfort.

"So, what's the long-term prognosis?" someone asked from the back.

Sandy shook her head. "None at this point. The neurologist told me it can go either way. He said he's seen patients older and frailer than Carl come in with injuries like this and heal up in a matter of days. But he also said there's the chance that we're looking at permanent disability." She glanced around, her eyes shining in the harsh light from the fixture overhead. "And I may as well come out and say it, but we need to all brace ourselves for the fact that Carl might not recover at all."

Murmurs of dissent broke out across the room until Sandy shushed everyone. "Now I'm trying to keep this from Woong. Lord knows that boy's had enough to worry about to last several lifetimes over. He's with his daddy now, and the detective's stopping by soon. Going to ask Woong some questions. There's a chance my boy saw who went into his daddy's office before the attack. But let's remember, we didn't come here to gossip or speculate. I only wanted to share what's been going on so we all know better how to direct our prayers. Now, we're here to talk to God, and that's just what I intend to do. But before we start, I want to say something, and because I know you love and respect my husband, I ask you to listen carefully.

"Carl and me have recognized for years that our days are numbered and that only God himself knows when our time to pass will come. You've heard Carl say so himself, each and every one of you. He's not the least bit scared of dying because he knows that when God calls him home, nothing can stand between him and his eternal reward, not modern medicine or heroic measures or even our steadfast love for each other will hold him back.

"Carl's got a living will. He makes no effort to hide that, and he's made it clear for decades that he doesn't want to just survive indefinitely on life support. Now, don't get yourselves too worked up yet. I've showed the doctor his will, and I've talked with both the social worker and the chaplain here at Providence, and all four of us are in agreement that in this instance, Carl would want us to try to do what we can to save his life. That man's been given a mission from God, a mission he's labored at tirelessly for decades, and I know for a fact that he doesn't consider his work on earth to be finished. But I also know that if it comes down to the brain damage being so severe that he couldn't make it without all kinds of outside measures keeping his body alive, there's no way my husband would wish to postpone his homecoming in that sort of situation.

"I'm not saying this to get anybody upset, and I'm not asking for suggestions or opinions here. Carl's wishes are quite clear, it's all documented and signed, and that's how I'm going to base all my decisions for his care if it comes down to it. We're not talking about pulling the plug. That's not even in the equation at this point. The doctor wants to redo the brain scan in three or four days. Whether or not we see improvement then will determine the next course of action.

"So here's what I'm asking for, friends. I don't pretend to know God's will in this situation. Heaven knows I've asked, but the Holy Spirit's either quiet, or my love for my husband and my desire to see him healed is getting in the way of me hearing clearly from the Lord. First and foremost, I want our prayers to be that God's will be done. Nothing more, nothing less. If God wants to miraculously touch my husband to stop any further injury and to heal the part of his brain that's already been damaged, then come, sweet Jesus, and work your miracles in Carl's mind and body. But if that's not the case, if this really is my husband's invitation to pass into glory, I'd like to ask God to answer my husband's wish and make that so clear that nothing could stop him from rushing into his Savior's arms. On a strictly human level, I'm asking that one way or the other Carl's suffering would not be unnecessarily prolonged, and of course you know that Woong and all our other children and grandchildren are in desperate need of our prayers and our support at this time."

Kennedy glanced around the room. Sandy's words

sounded so morbid. The thought of someone as strong and robust as Carl ending up with such severe brain trauma was grotesque, and yet the room filled with an unexpected peace even before the praying began.

Sandy started, but she got choked up before she could even get past her very first "Thy will be done." At that point, someone else took up where she left off, and around the room the prayers rose and fell and were passed on to others like a synchronized dance. Kennedy wasn't comfortable speaking in front of such a large group, but nobody seemed to mind or even notice when some people prayed out loud and others only joined in silent agreement.

Kennedy had never experienced anything like this. She'd encountered people she considered prayer warriors before, like Dominic whose prayer over her had stopped a full-fledged panic attack the very first night they met. Or Grandma Lucy, the bold and faithful stranger Kennedy sat next to in an airplane on the way to her first trip to Alaska. Sandy had interceded over her dozens of times, and Kennedy and Willow tried to end each day with a short time of prayer together. But still nothing she'd encountered in the past came close to this. She'd experienced peace before while she prayed. She'd experienced overwhelming waves of comfort or the certainty of God's love or the glory of his divine presence.

But this prayer meeting in the overstuffed conference room was different. Yes, there was peace. Yes, there was comfort even though at least a third of the people present were crying or had shed tears at some point during the meeting. But there was something else too. A power. An undeniable surge of energy that raced around the room. Kennedy noticed that even though the first few people who prayed asked God humbly for his will to be done, now nearly everybody who spoke was beseeching God for Carl's full and perfect healing. Kennedy found herself surprised by the confidence surging in her own spirit. She'd never felt such a burning fire, such a sincere conviction that she could ask God right now to do the impossible, to heal Carl and grant him a complete recovery, and that he would answer her fully. Her heart raced faster, and she wondered if a nurse was about to enter the room to tell them Carl had woken up from his coma and was breathing perfectly well now on his own.

It could have been forty minutes, it could have been two hours later, but at some point, as if by general consensus, everyone stopped praying. The ones who'd kept their eyes closed now opened them. Bowed heads lifted and looked around the room. Sandy sat in a corner, comforted by at least a dozen loving arms stretching out to embrace her. She smiled at the group and said, "I suppose that's *amen*."

Kennedy glanced at Willow. What now? The prayers had been so sincere. The faith so real. Should they all go check on Carl? Would they see him sitting up in bed sharing corny Bible jokes with his son?

Sandy rose. She looked half a foot taller now and even more stately than normal. "This was such a blessing. It just means the world to me and brings me so much hope and encouragement that you all joined with me. I hate to pray and run, but I really should go check on Woong. I'll update the prayer chain tonight, and I'll do it sooner if Carl's condition changes at all between now and then. Thanks again for praying with me." She glided gracefully out the door.

So that was it?

Willow looked just as surprised. "What now?" she asked.

Kennedy shrugged. Some of the people she'd recently prayed with were already gathering their bags and buttoning their sweaters, while others formed small pockets and began to talk to one another.

Willow grabbed Kennedy by the arm. "Come on. There's something I want to show you before we leave."

CHAPTER 24

Kennedy had no idea why Willow was dragging her down hallway after hallway or why they had to take two different elevators. By the time Willow slowed down to look at a map of the hospital, they were already four towers away from the ICU where they'd prayed for Carl.

"Can you just tell me what we're doing?" Kennedy wasn't in the mood for games. Sandy's words about Carl now sat ominously in her gut like a spoiled dinner. Words like *permanent disability* crashed around her cerebral cortex like the wild, unquenchable flames of *Fahrenheit 451*.

Willow looked back in the direction they'd just come from. Were they lost? She studied the map again. "Ok, it should be right down this hall. Or maybe that one."

"Where are we going?" Kennedy hated to admit how whiney she sounded.

"You'll see when we get there."

Kennedy's feet ached from clunking those awkward heels all around Providence. She struggled to keep up with her roommate, who finally stopped in front of a small plaque hanging up outside a closed door.

"What's this?" Kennedy asked. The room wasn't marked, and there were no windows. It was more likely a janitorial closet than an office. What had Willow planned?

"Look." She pointed at the plaque on the wall. "That's what I wanted you to see."

When Kennedy saw the name and read the inscription, she realized why this hall felt familiar. It was different now, the construction newer, the whole section remodeled since last spring. But here they were. Outside the same room where she'd been trapped the last day she and Dominic had been together.

Willow's hand rested on the doorknob. "Do you want to go in?"

Kennedy shook her head. She wasn't ready. Not for this.

Willow frowned. "I'm sorry. Was this too hard of a surprise? Should I have told you about it first?"

Kennedy blinked and tried to read the inscription again through her blurry field of vision. *Dominic Martinez, Courageous Chaplain, Devoted Servant.* John 15:13 was written across the bottom. *Greater love has no one than this: to lay down one's life for one's friends.*

Willow wrapped an arm around her. "I just thought

you'd like to see it. And you know, maybe go in there. It doesn't have to be today. But the two of you never got the chance to say good-bye."

Kennedy swallowed. Her throat felt like it had been prodded with a red-hot fire poker.

"Want me to give you a little time here alone?" Willow asked.

Kennedy shook her head.

"Too much?" Willow whispered.

She nodded.

"Should we go?" Willow held her around the waist and led her back down the hall.

The suffocating constriction in Kennedy's chest widened like a gaping chasm. A black hole whose event horizon kept expanding infinitesimally. There were days when she thought she was doing so well. Days when she was sure she'd trudged her way through the deepest caverns of grief. But after the intense pain came the aching. The missing. The emptiness that sometimes she was certain nothing could fill, the wound without balm. He should have been here today, should have joined in interceding for Carl's healing. Kennedy had never met someone with a prayer life like his.

Would it always be like this? Always good-bye, no matter how much time had passed, time that was promised to heal all wounds? Would she always feel so lost?

But then she could go days on end hardly mourning at all. Good days. Busy days. Filled with schoolwork and reading and lab reports. Should she feel guilty that she was trying to move on? Did the fact that she was still functioning — although now with the help of prescription medicine — somehow diminish the loss she'd suffered? If she and Dominic had been even closer, would her recovery take that much longer?

Was it wrong for her to want to live again? Laugh again? Love again?

Was it even possible?

"Come on." Willow led her toward the elevator. "Now that you know it's here, you can come back any time you want, ok?"

"Ok." Kennedy wasn't sure if she'd ever be ready to face the memories flooding this corridor in Providence again, but when the time came, *if* the time came, she knew she had a friend who would walk with her through the grief.

Who would help her say good-bye.

CHAPTER 25

The phone rang almost the same instant they stepped outside of Providence Hospital. "Oh." Willow reached into her purse. "I forgot. I've been carrying around your cell all morning." She handed it to Kennedy. "Here you go."

Kennedy didn't recognize the number. "Hello?"

"This is Adell. Are you free to talk?"

Actually, her professor's timing couldn't be worse, but Kennedy didn't say so. "Yeah, this is great." She put her hand over the receiver and whispered to Willow, "It's my chemistry professor."

Adell had never been the type to squander words. "I'm calling to confirm you got my previous message. The one about not coming into lab today."

"Yes." Kennedy wasn't sure how her voice was supposed to sound right now. Hurt? Stoic? Disappointed?

"Well …" Adell let out a small cough. "I don't mind going on record stating that I'm in complete disagreement with Dr. Faber on this one."

Kennedy wondered what to say. Did Adell want to vent about her colleague? Did she expect Kennedy to join in her complaints against the department head who'd barred Kennedy from her lab?

"Regardless," Adell went on, "it's not to be helped. He's made up his mind, at least for today. I can't promise you your position back, but I did manage to get him to agree to a meeting."

"Meeting?"

Kennedy could almost taste the impatience in her professor's voice. "Yes. A meeting. My office, this afternoon at three. You'll be there." It was far more of a statement than a question.

Kennedy checked the time. It was only a few minutes after noon. "Yeah, I can make it."

"See that you do." Adell ended the call before saying anything else.

Kennedy slipped her phone into her pocket, aware of Willow's quizzical eyes on her. "Problems again with the professor?"

Kennedy shrugged. She didn't want to get into any details. What she really needed was a nap. Who would have thought a prayer meeting could be so exhausting?

Willow unlocked her car, but Kennedy stopped when her

phone rang again. Had Adell forgotten to tell her something? She glanced at the screen.

"Hi, Sandy." Kennedy paused with her hand on the car door. Willow stopped too and stared openly.

"Kennedy, thank God I got hold of you." Sandy was breathless. Fear iced over Kennedy's heart when Sandy asked, "Is Woong with you by any chance?"

"No." Kennedy looked around the parking lot as if he were about to jump out from behind one of the cars and shout *surprise*. "No," she repeated. "I haven't seen him all morning."

"Oh, dear. I was afraid of that."

Kennedy had already started walking back toward the hospital. Willow was right behind her.

Sandy mumbled something, but Kennedy couldn't make it out. "What's that?"

"I'm sorry, sweetie," Sandy answered. "I'm here with the detective. You've probably already left the hospital by now, haven't you?"

"No. We're in the parking garage, but we're on our way back in. We'll help you look around for Woong." Kennedy was nearly jogging now, platform shoes or not. "Do you think he wandered or something?"

Sandy sighed on the other line. "I wish it were that simple."

CHAPTER 26

"So Woong's missing?" Willow had picked up on enough of Kennedy's conversation with Sandy to be worried. The girls sprinted toward the elevator that would take them to the ICU. Kennedy prayed she wouldn't twist an ankle in those heeled sandals.

"Yeah. I don't know what happened." Kennedy stared at every strange face she passed, wondering if Woong would be among them.

Willow rubbed her back when they got on the elevator. "I'm sure he's just fine."

Kennedy wished she could borrow some of her friend's optimism.

When they reached the ICU, Sandy was at the front desk, surrounded by several nurses, security officers, and Detective Drisklay, who raised his Styrofoam cup in expressionless greeting when he saw Kennedy come near.

Sandy rushed toward her and wrapped her up in a hug. "I'm so glad you came back, darling. I declare it's a miracle

I'm still standing. That's how rattled my nerves are." She hugged Willow next. "You two are such sweethearts to be here right now. You're not skipping classes or missing anything important, are you?"

Kennedy shook her head and tried not to think of the lab she wasn't teaching this afternoon. "We're fine. What's going on here? What happened to Woong?"

Soft wrinkles furrowed around Sandy's eyes. "Oh, it's terrible, honey. Just terrible."

"Do you think he got lost looking for a snack or something?" Willow asked with an awkward chuckle that was hardly convincing.

"No, nothing like that, love." Sandy walked back up toward the desk. The security officers and nurses spread out in different directions. Only Drisklay remained, sipping his coffee as if he were an actor in some TV commercial for cheap Styrofoam cups.

Sandy put her hands up to her temples. "I think maybe the detective should fill you in on the details. My mind's just spinning and racing, and I can hardly focus on anything right about now."

Drisklay was scowling at them, an expression which Kennedy had figured out years ago simply indicated he was alive and breathing. "Miss Stern," he mumbled without acknowledging Willow right next to her.

"What happened?" her roommate asked.

Drisklay took a noisy sip of coffee. "That's the thousand-dollar question, isn't it?"

"Well, what do you guess happened?" Kennedy tried.

The detective set his Styrofoam cup on the nurses' station. "Here's what we know. This morning the boy mentioned that he saw someone going into his dad's office at the church a few minutes before the attack. Said he looked a little familiar, but he didn't know who it was. His mother called, asked if it was relevant to the case, and I said I'd come right over and we'd try to reconstruct what the suspect looked like. She asked me to wait since you were all doing your little kumbaya prayer thing for the pastor, so I said I'd come at noon.

"In the meantime, while all you folks were busy talking with the unseen Almighty, the boy was sitting by his father's bedside, reading joke books to a coma patient. That's when someone came and told the nurse he was the detective here to talk to the boy. The nurse called the kid out, kid acted like he recognized the man, and the nurse said they could talk in the break room since all you folks were so conveniently taking up the regular meeting room.

"Problem is, whoever that man was, he obviously wasn't

me, and now he and the kid are gone. Security's pulling footage right now. Hospital's going on lockdown, but if you ask me, it won't do a gram of good. That man and the kid made their escape a full half hour before you all stopped asking some invisible deity to heal the pastor."

"It's all my fault, I'm afraid," Sandy added. "I came out to check on Woong, and the nurse told me he was already in a meeting with the detective. I should have gone right then to see him, but the doctor stopped by, and I had some questions for him about my husband, and …" She shook her head. "I should have never left Woong in that room alone for so long."

Willow wrapped her arm around Sandy's shoulder. "You had no way to know something like this would happen."

"No, but he should have been with me. He should have been at that prayer meeting. Might have done his spirit good, too, listening to all them folks loving his father."

Willow shook her head. "Woong wanted to be by his dad. He was doing exactly what he was supposed to be doing, just like you were. This isn't anybody's fault."

"Except, of course, the perpetrator's," Drisklay added in his usual lifeless monotone.

"Ok." Kennedy looked around her. The security officers

must be sweeping the whole building or something. She didn't see any of them. "How can we help? Do we start going room to room? Knocking on doors? What?"

Drisklay shook his head. "That kid's as far out of here as a baseball in the Polo Grounds with the Bambino up to bat."

Kennedy tried to decipher what he'd just said while Willow snapped, "A little more positive thinking, maybe?"

Drisklay held up his hand. "Hey, you three want to go back in the conference room and talk to God about it some more, be my guest. Or you could start by listing the names of all the men who came this morning to your little prayer session."

"What would be the point of that?" Willow asked with slightly less edge in her voice.

"The man who came in here wasn't a stranger. The boy knew him. Seems to me a pretty likely guess he started out at your prayer meeting, waited until you were all in your holy huddle and not paying any attention, and he snuck out and kidnapped the kid."

Kennedy wanted to cover Sandy's ears. Who did the detective think he was using language like that? Woong hadn't been kidnapped. He'd been … he'd been …

She let out her breath.

Maybe Drisklay had the right idea after all. Maybe they should focus on the people at the prayer meeting. At least it was something proactive they could do. Try to get Woong back.

Kennedy turned to the detective. “Got any paper?”

CHAPTER 27

Fifteen minutes later, they were seated in the small conference room around Drisklay and his list of ten men they could remember being at the morning's prayer meeting. "Now," Drisklay announced, "we figure out who'd want to take the kid."

Willow ran her fingers through her hair. "You know, I've been thinking, and I've got an idea that makes pretty good sense."

Drisklay leaned forward. Kennedy couldn't tell from his expression if he was eager for any sort of lead on this case or if he was surprised that a college girl with neon-green hair could have anything even partially resembling a good idea.

"All right." Willow paused dramatically. "So this morning Woong told his mom he remembered seeing someone go into his dad's office. That's probably the same guy who attacked Carl." She glanced at Drisklay, who remained expressionless. "Ok, and then Sandy told the people in the prayer meeting that Woong was going to meet with the detective. We all heard her say so."

Kennedy nodded, clearly remembering the incident.

"So here's what I'm thinking." Willow got up from her chair and started to pace, pointing her pen in the air. "What if the same guy who attacked Carl was in the prayer meeting this morning? He heard Sandy say Woong was going to meet with the detective, got scared, and came up with this plan to get Woong out of the hospital before he had a chance to tell the police what he knew?" She stopped, smiling broadly and clearly enjoying her dramatic role.

Drisklay raised an eyebrow. Kennedy wasn't sure she'd ever seen him put that much expression into his face before. "You come up with that all on your own?"

Kennedy's cheeks warmed up on her roommate's behalf.

"I think that's a very possible explanation." Sandy reached out and petted Willow on the arm like she was a puppy who'd just learned a new trick. "I think we should move forward with Willow's assumption."

Drisklay muttered something under his breath, but Kennedy could only make out the last half: "... made it all the way into Harvard."

Willow sat down, clearly less sure of herself now but still

wanting to help. "So which of these people would have any reason to hurt Carl in the first place?"

Sandy shook her head. "I just don't know. Carl and me decided years ago that when he was having issues with folks at the church, he would talk to me about it, but we used a strict no-names policy. It made it easier for me that way. If Jack cheats on Jill, and they go to Carl about it for counseling, Carl comes home and tells me there's a couple struggling from the consequences of infidelity so I can pray for them. But he doesn't tell me who Jack is, and he doesn't tell me who Jill is. I like it that way because when folks know that's our policy, Jill doesn't feel like she has to tiptoe around me, and Jack doesn't feel like I'm judging him. If folks want to come to me and tell me what's going on, they can do that, or sometimes Carl and I meet with them together, so of course at that point I know who they are." She glanced at the list again. "But I don't think I've met with any of these men."

"By the way, why are we only focusing on the men?" Willow asked. "Isn't it just as possible that a woman could have attacked Carl for some reason? I mean, you hear about churches all the time where the pastor counsels the wife to stay with an abusive husband. What if it was something like that, and she got mad at Carl for putting her and her family in danger?"

"Oh, no, dear." Sandy rested her hand on Willow's arm. "Carl's never been the kind to tell women they just have to roll over and take it in cases like that. He always advocates they get themselves and their children — if there are any children involved — to safety. He's very adamant about that because he's seen too many woman stay in horrible situations in the name of biblical submission."

Drisklay was staring at Sandy and Willow with wide, unbelieving eyes, but Kennedy suspected she was the only one who noticed. "A much simpler explanation," he offered, "is that the individual masquerading as a police detective was male."

"Oh." Willow stared at her fingernails which she'd recently painted orange in celebration of autumn. "That makes sense."

"Should we make a list of any of the women who were here that we think could pull off an impressive male impersonation, or are we content with the names we've got?" Drisklay asked.

"No, we're good," Willow answered, somewhat sheepishly.

Drisklay's comment reminded Kennedy of a problem she'd been mulling over. "Now that you mention it though, how can we be sure these are all the names here? I mean, it's not like we took roll or anything. And it was so crowded. Some people could have come in late or left early …" She caught Drisklay's scowl and tried to make her point more concisely. "All I'm saying is we might not have a comprehensive list to work with."

Drisklay gave a brisk nod. "We've got a security team pulling up footage as we speak. It won't be a perfect image, but it might fill in some blanks."

Sandy was shaking her head. "Sweet Jesus, you're really stretching my faith this time, Lord, and I don't mean to sound ungrateful, but I don't know how much more worry my poor soul can bear."

"Excuse my lack of religious fervor, but I'd bet your energy would be better spent talking to your friends here about which of these men would have reason to assault your husband and kidnap your son."

Kennedy kept her eyes low, but Willow stood up from her chair. "Excuse me, Detective Barkley or Berkley or whatever your name is, but while we're talking about gambling, I've got a wager for you. I'm betting that you've never had a spouse on life support, and you've never had a child kidnapped right out from under your nose. So until you've gone through a fraction of what Sandy has, my *bet* is that you'll want to keep your mouth shut about things you know absolutely nothing about."

Nobody spoke. Drisklay cleared his throat and picked up his coffee cup. "I'm going to see about that security footage. I expect some pertinent information about each individual listed by the time I get back."

CHAPTER 28

Kennedy stared while Drisklay shut the door nosily behind him.

"Good riddance," Willow mumbled.

Sandy took her by the hand. "Now, sweetheart, it was kind of you to stand up for me like that, and I know you did it with kind intentions, but is yelling at that detective the best way to love him into the kingdom of God?"

"I'm not trying to love anyone into anywhere right now," Willow replied, then added more softly, "but I'm sorry if I embarrassed you."

Sandy reached over and hugged her. "It's not me you need to apologize to, dear. But there now. As curmudgeonly as that detective is, he knows what he's doing. I was wrong to allow myself to get so emotional while he was here, but he's right about one thing. We need to focus on these names if we want to figure out who may have wanted to hurt my Carl. It's the best shot we've got at finding Woong. So ..." She put the piece of paper out in front of her. "This is what we've got."

Kennedy looked over the names. She only recognized two or three.

Sandy stared at the list. Kennedy hated to interrupt but finally admitted, "I'm not sure how helpful Willow and I are going to be at this."

"Nonsense." Sandy smoothed out the list again, as if touching the paper itself might give her insight into the motives of the men whose names were written there. "We'll find our answer here. There's got to be something. Now, let me think. Scott Phillips, he's a dear of a saint. Spent the past ten years on the mission field and now that he's back Stateside we have him over for lunch sometimes after church. He loves the Lord and has his heart set on marrying this young girl he met, and I declare he doesn't have a violent bone in his body. Now." She moved her graceful finger down the page. "John August is a newer member of the church. Got saved just a year ago, I think, but Carl and I know him pretty well. We met him when he served at our table when we went out for our anniversary last year, and we struck up a friendship there. He accepted Christ a few months later, and Carl's been discipling him since then. They meet pretty regularly still, and I have no reason to suspect there's any tension between them. But you know who'd have a better idea for these things than me?" Sandy's eyes lit. "Let's call Dawn, Carl's secretary. She handles all his appointments, knows who he's meeting when. I think if we explained to her why it's so important, she'd be willing to listen to our list of names and go through them with us."

A minute later, the secretary from St. Margaret's Church was on speaker phone. Sandy explained in a rather roundabout way why they needed information about the different men listed, and Dawn seemed willing to help. Two of them Dawn had never met, which made it likely they'd never visited Carl in his office, so for now, the women decided to focus on the other eight.

"All right." Sandy looked at the names again. "What do you know about Simon Golding?"

Dawn paused for a moment. "Let's see. He comes in every so often. He and Carl …" She hesitated.

"I know this is hard," Sandy said. "You're so discreet, which is why Carl trusts you with everything. I know you hate the thought of gossip, but this information may lead us to my son."

"I know." Dawn cleared her throat. "I know. Ok, so Simon and Carl meet maybe once a month, once every other month. He's having some struggles. I don't know all the details." She lowered her voice. "He and Carl are going through the blue book."

Sandy's eyes widened. "Oh. That. Ok, and you don't hear them fight ever?"

"Not a peep."

"When was the last time he was in?" Sandy asked.

"Let me check." The sound of Dawn's fingers typing on her keyboard carried over through the speaker phone.

Kennedy waited, wondering what this blue book was that Dawn and Sandy seemed so eager to not discuss.

"He hasn't been in since August," Dawn finally answered.

"Ok. Probably not him." Sandy crossed out his name and then pointed to the list with her pen. "Next we've got George Winston."

Dawn took in a deep breath. "His case is pretty basic. Grief counseling after his wife died, and that's about it. Once or twice he's brought the kids in with him, but they're teens, and as far as I can tell they're handling her passing as well as can be expected."

Kennedy didn't know the family they were referring to and wondered if she and Willow would be better off searching for Woong room to room. But, of course, Drisklay was right. If the abductor's goal was to keep Woong from telling the detective what he knew, there's no way the two of them would still be here at Providence.

Sandy and Dawn discussed the personal lives of several other men in the church. As it turns out, one other was going through *the blue book* with Carl, and like before Sandy rushed to finish that conversation as quickly as possible.

"So is that everyone?" Dawn finally asked.

"Well, Jackson stopped by." Sandy let out a little laugh, even though Kennedy didn't know what was funny.

"He did?"

"It must have been his work break or something," Sandy said. "I know how busy the office keeps him. It was nice he got a free minute to sneak away and pray with us. I know his schedule isn't easy for the two of you."

"Yeah," Dawn muttered. "Well, did you ever wonder if maybe it wasn't one of these men at all? Maybe it was a coincidence that what happened took place during the prayer meeting. Or maybe someone was waiting for a distraction."

Sandy frowned. "It's possible, I suppose. I hate to ask you to betray confidences like this, but is there anyone else you can think of who's given Carl trouble lately?"

Dawn was quiet for so long, Kennedy began to wonder if the call had been disconnected.

"I know it's not easy to talk about," Sandy prodded, "but please. This is my son who's missing."

"It's ok," Dawn assured her. "I'm just trying to think of the best way to put this. I don't want to give you one more thing to worry about. You've been through so much."

"Right now, I want to know everything so when the detective comes back, we can give him a full picture of who may or may not have wanted to harm my husband."

Dawn let out a noisy sigh. "All right, then. Well, I hate to bring it up because I know you and Carl have already dealt with a lot because of the Truth Warriors event coming up. But it's more than the media and the college students around town who've gotten upset. I'm not sure Carl told you about it. He didn't want to worry you, but there have been quite a few women from the church pretty outspoken against the conference."

"All this about a men's retreat?" Sandy asked.

Dawn cleared her throat. "It's more than that. Some women feel like St. Margaret's is already too patriarchal in its structure."

Sandy straightened her spine. "You know my husband has the utmost respect for everyone."

"Yes," Dawn replied, "but he also is very conservative in his interpretation of Scripture, and some women worry that he takes certain passages from the Bible too far."

Kennedy could tell that Sandy wanted to reply but was restraining herself.

"I can only imagine how hard it must be as the pastor's wife to know there are people upset with the way things are, but with a church the size of St. Margaret's, there's no way everyone will be happy."

"Just what kind of complaints have you heard?" Sandy asked.

"Actually, I have a list of several grievances that some women wanted Carl to bring up at the next elders' meeting."

"I never knew about a list," Sandy remarked.

"Yeah, well, your husband likes to protect you from church politics as much as he can."

Kennedy thought she heard some sort of hidden barb beneath the words, but she couldn't be exactly sure.

Sandy let out her breath. "So this list, do you think there's any way it has to do with Carl's attack?"

"I really wouldn't know."

Sandy ran her hand across the floral pattern of her skirt. "Well, why don't you tell me a few of the points so I at least have something of an idea of what to share with the detective. I honestly can't believe how anyone from St. Margaret's could accuse my husband of treating the women of our church unfairly."

“You sure this will be helpful?” Dawn asked doubtfully.

“I have no clue. But you know more about it than I do, so it’s hard for me to make any judgment at this point in time.”

Kennedy glanced at Willow and wondered if her roommate was also picking up on a hint of animosity between the two women.

“All right.” Dawn sighed. “First of all, there have been some complaints about the way the elder board handled the Gordons. You remember the missionaries who came to speak last month.”

“Yes, I remember.”

“The couple made it clear when we invited them that Mrs. Gordon was the one involved in the direct, day-to-day ministry, and her husband was the one who oversaw the behind-the-scenes details of their work.”

“I fail to see what objections an advocate of women’s rights would raise to a situation like that,” Sandy stated.

“They didn’t object to their situation. What upset them was that it was only Mr. Gordon who presented in church, even though his wife was obviously the one with the greater field experience and knowledge of the region. But unless you went to the separate event just for women Tuesday morning, you wouldn’t have been able to hear a word she had to say about her ministry overseas."

"So the women of St. Margaret's are so offended by that they're taking their complaints to the elder board?" There was a tremor in Sandy's voice.

"It's not just that, but since you asked, there's quite a large list of things like this. Some might sound petty, like how it's only men who read the opening Scripture passages on Sunday mornings, but they add up. One woman sent me an email to pass on anonymously that she's afraid to say anything in Carl's Sunday school class because she feels like women aren't supposed to talk in church."

"That's ridiculous. Carl would never preach something like that."

"No, but where does the line get drawn? If a woman can't teach an adult Sunday School class, can she raise an objection or offer a differing viewpoint, or will some people feel threatened because she's assumed a teaching position even for those few minutes? If ninety percent of the people the pastor asks to open the service in prayer are men, might that send the message to women that their prayers are somehow less important?"

"Carl has a Scriptural reason behind every decision he's made for our church." Sandy's voice was defensive. Kennedy wondered if it would be best for her and Willow to head out. It didn't sound like this conversation would lead them to Woong's abductor or Carl's attacker anytime soon.

"Well, you'd have to have Carl show me the chapter and verse that says women shouldn't pass around an offering plate. I'm not here to argue the Bible with you, Sandy. I'm really not. But I've heard these women's concerns, and I've talked with several of them firsthand, and some are deeply wounded."

"I'm very sorry to hear that. Carl never mentioned any complaints like this to me."

"Yeah, well, we both know how he likes to shield you from church politics as much as possible. And I'm sorry for burdening you with all of this. You know how much I enjoy working with your husband. I personally have no complaints."

"Well, I'm glad to hear that, and I understand that you're only the messenger here. I'm so deeply indebted to you for the way you serve our congregation and encourage my husband. You and I know better than anyone else at St. Margaret's how that man needs full-time help to stay organized and on task, and I thank God nearly every day that he raised you up for that purpose, and I'm grateful to you for all the time and energy you sacrifice."

The conversation probably would have turned mushy if Detective Drisklay hadn't chosen that moment to bang the doors open and stride in.

Oblivious to Sandy's phone call, he tossed a folder onto the table in front of them. "Well, looks like security found our perp."

CHAPTER 29

Kennedy stared at the image of a tall man walking beside Woong out the hospital exit.

"Who's he?" Willow asked the question Kennedy was eager to have answered.

Sandy stared at the image. "That's Jackson Phelps," she answered in a lifeless voice. "Dawn's husband." She shook her head. "Dawn's the church secretary," she told the detective.

"Volunteer secretary, from what I gather," he inserted.

Sandy hadn't stopped shaking her head.

Drisklay took a sip of coffee. "Now that we know who we're looking for, our chances of finding the kid just went from basically impossible to likely. If we get even more information, if for example we're able to go over to St. Margaret's and ask his wife where her husband might be, if we can coerce her to tell us what she ..."

"Coercing will be unnecessary, officer." The tinny voice from Sandy's cell phone made Kennedy jump. Willow raised her penciled eyebrows and let out a low, whispered,

"Dude," and Sandy gasped aloud. Drisklay was the only one who didn't seem fazed by the unexpected interruption. "This is Mrs. Phelps I presume?"

"Yes." Dawn's voice from Sandy's speaker was strong and somewhat stoic. "And whom am I addressing?"

"Detective Drisklay. I take it you overheard our conversation about your husband?"

"Yes, sir."

"Do you have anything helpful that you'd like to add?"

There was a pause on the other end.

Kennedy hoped that Dawn would cooperate. "It'd be easier to talk this through in person," she finally said.

Drisklay scowled. "No time. You do realize that your husband has just kidnapped a child, don't you?"

"You have actual pictures to prove it?"

"We do," Drisklay answered.

Dawn's voice was hopeful when she asked quietly, "Sandy?"

Sandy nodded her head at her cell phone. "I'm afraid so. The pictures couldn't be much clearer. That's Jackson, and he and Woong …" She didn't finish her sentence.

"All right." Drisklay took a slow sip from his Styrofoam cup. "It's time for you to tell us everything you know. Starting with where your husband might be taking the kid."

CHAPTER 30

"You want to know where my husband is, you show me those pictures yourself." Dawn's voice was as resolute as Woong's whenever he was preparing to throw a full-fledged temper tantrum. It got softer for just a minute when she added, "It's not you I don't trust, Sandy. It's the whole system. If that detective wants information, he's got to show me those photographs, and then I'll tell him anything he wants to know."

The vein in Drisklay's forearm bulged slightly as he picked up his cup. "No good. Every minute lost puts that kid at even more risk."

"Sir, I don't know you, and you sure as anything don't know me, and that means we've got to trust each other. Trust goes both ways, see. My husband for all his faults is not a dangerous man. Not in the least. You ask Sandy, and she'll tell you the exact same thing."

Drisklay's tone never changed. "I don't know what dictionary you use over there at that church you work at, but in the one I use, a *dangerous* man is someone who lies and kidnaps a child. You talk about trust. Well I can talk about trust, too. For example, I want to trust that you're not complicit in your husband's crimes, but unless I get some evidence toward that end, well, we've got ourselves a problem."

Sandy leaned toward the phone. "Dawn, love, do you have any idea where your husband might be fixing to take my son? I'm asking you mother to mother now, and I hope I might say friend to friend. Do you know where they might be going?" Sandy ignored Drisklay's well-rehearsed glare of death.

"Yes, I do," Dawn answered. "As soon as I overheard that detective — you'll pardon me, sir, if I forget your name for the moment — but as soon as I heard him saying it was my Jackson in the photo, I knew where he was off to. I'm home now and just confirmed it." Dawn ended as if that was all there was to say about it. Kennedy leaned forward, waiting to hear more.

Drisklay glowered at the phone for a silent moment before finally asking, "Well, care to enlighten the rest of us with that little bit of information?" Sandy clasped her hands in front of her and started to whisper a prayer. All Kennedy could make out was, "Please, sweet Jesus."

On the other end of the line, Dawn let out a heavy sigh. "His cousin owns a place near Salisbury. A little cabin, way out in the woods. Lets us use it anytime we want. We've even got our own key. When you said you'd identified Jackson on the security cameras, I checked to see if my suspicions were right. The key's gone. Now, I can't promise you it was in its usual spot this morning when I woke up, but I'd say it's a pretty reasonable guess that Jackson's on his way there. I'm so sorry, Sandy. I never thought he'd do anything like this. I would have stopped him. God is my witness, I would have done anything to keep him from acting out like this if I had the smallest inkling of suspicion. And I will do everything in my power to help you get your son back safe and sound."

Sandy nodded and wiped a tear off her cheek but didn't say anything.

Drisklay cleared his throat. "I'm glad to see you've finally come to your senses and decided to cooperate. Where in Salisbury is this cabin you mentioned? How far away? How do we get there?"

Dawn sniffed loudly enough for it to carry over the speakerphone. Drisklay grimaced.

"It's a little over an hour from here. I can meet you at the church and show you where to go."

"No." Drisklay pulled out his notebook with a scowl. "You tell me now, so I can relay directions to my men. Then you come with us in case we need you to talk some sense into that spouse of yours."

He straightened his shirt and tossed his cup into the trash. "Let's get this woman her son back."

CHAPTER 31

"You're sure you're going to be ok?" Willow asked as Kennedy lowered herself into the passenger seat of Sandy's Honda.

"Yeah." She offered her roommate what she hoped was a reassuring smile. "Remember, I don't have to go to my lab class today. I'm as free as a bird."

The tender concern didn't leave Willow's face. "You know that's not what I'm talking about. I mean Woong, Carl, everything with Dominic earlier. You sure you want to go? Nobody would blame you for sitting back and praying from the sidelines this time."

Kennedy shook her head. "I've got to do this." It was hard to explain. It wasn't just that Kennedy wanted to be there as a support and comfort to Sandy. Of course that was a large part of it, but there was more to it than that. For starters, Woong was something between a cousin and a little brother to her. Kennedy had grown up as an only child in a family without even distant relatives close to her age. She'd had friends at school but never that kind of intimacy and togetherness she always imagined would come from a larger family. Besides, she knew what it was like to be abducted. She knew how scared Woong must be. Even if all she did was sit next to Sandy and pray with her for Woong's safe return, she had to be doing something.

Willow leaned down and gave her a noisy peck right next to her cheek in classic New England style. "I'll be praying for you," she whispered.

"You want to come?" Kennedy asked, trying not to sound too pushy.

Willow shook her head. "I'm actually kind of worried about Nick. I haven't heard from him all day. He's taking this whole thing harder than he wants any of us to guess. I'm not sure he even knows about Woong yet. I've been leaving him messages, but he's not returning my texts."

"Well, try not to worry." Kennedy offered one last smile as her roommate shut the door.

Sandy sat down next to her. "You sure you want to come along?" she asked. "God knows I'm happy for the company, but with all you've been through …"

Kennedy didn't want to rehash the same conversation she'd just had with Willow. "I'm sure."

Sandy turned the car key with one hand and wiped her

cheek with the other. It pained Kennedy to see her friend and mentor suffering so greatly.

"Want me to drive?" Kennedy asked.

Sandy shook her head. "No, dear. This will be good for me, give me something to focus on. And I'm sorry, but that detective talks in such a monotone, and I'm so worried over poor little Woong that I'm afraid I only caught every other word he said. Is Dawn going with him, or do we pick her up at her house?"

"No." Kennedy was glad she'd decided to come along. She'd never seen Sandy so frail before. "Dawn will meet us at the church since it's on the way. Drisklay and his men are already headed to the cabin."

"Think it's going to be dangerous?" Sandy asked as she pulled out of Providence parking lot.

Kennedy tried not to recall the details of her own kidnapping her first year at Harvard. "I'm sure it's going to work out just fine."

Sandy was halfway to St. Margaret's Church before she turned off her praise and worship music. "Sometimes the newer songs are just too upbeat for me. Do you ever find that yourself?"

Kennedy hadn't been listening to the album. She'd been too busy worrying about Woong. Wondering what would go through the head of a child that young. He must be terrified. And after all he'd suffered growing up on the streets in Korea. Why did some people seem to be cursed with all the bad luck?

Sandy pointed to a small collection of CDs in the center console. "Somewhere in here I've got one called *Hymns of the Faith*. Do you see that one, darling?"

Kennedy thumbed through the albums until she found it. Once she put it in, she realized that Sandy was right. The bright, chipper choruses from the first CD had been entirely inappropriate for a day like this.

When peace like a river attendeth my way …

Kennedy thought back to the times she'd spent with Sandy. The Lindgren home was always such a respite, such a comfort to her. There was some kind of special blessing, an anointing on the house itself. Kennedy was sure of it. She'd never spent time at the Lindgrens' and failed to come away more relaxed than before. Only this time, it was Sandy who needed that peace and comfort.

When sorrows like sea billows roll.

Kennedy would have never understood what that phrase meant before last spring. Losing Dominic had been one of the most intense trials she'd ever suffered. And yet God was bringing her through it. Just like God would bring Sandy through the tempest raging around her today. The difference was that everything with Dominic happened so fast. Completely unexpected, which came with its own sort of emotional trauma, but there had been no pins-and-needles wait at the end. No uncertainty.

Poor Sandy was surrounded by nothing but uncertainty. Uncertainty regarding her husband as well as her son. Where was Woong? Kennedy hoped the detective was on the right track now. What if Dawn was wrong? What if her husband had no intention of taking Woong to that cabin? What if Woong was already …

No, she couldn't think like that. Especially now when Sandy needed her the most.

Whatever my lot, thou hast taught me to say, "It is well, it is well with my soul."

Sandy hummed along so quietly Kennedy wasn't entirely sure she could hear it. During the first instrumental break, Sandy whispered, "Thank you, sweet Jesus." Kennedy wondered if she would be like that someday. Serene in the face of fear. Calm in the midst of the storm.

When Kennedy first met her, Sandy appeared immune to sadness. But now Kennedy could discern the underlying heaviness, the body of grief that weighed down Sandy's spirit. And yet still she could hum softly along with her hymns or lift up her voice, quiet and weak though it was, to praise her Savior.

Kennedy had never met anyone else like her.

"I'm sorry I'm being such poor company," Sandy said when the song ended.

Kennedy smiled. "I was actually about to say the same thing myself, but I didn't want to interrupt your time of worship."

Sandy turned down her music. "It's a sweet gift to be able to wrap myself up in the love and peace of my heavenly Father. I don't know what I'd do without that comfort." She hummed along a little more when the next song started. "You know, I read an interesting devotional once on grief. Sent it to a foster daughter of mine whose baby stopped breathing right after birth and suffered some real bad brain damage. This article, it had a lot of good points, but the one that stood out to me most is how in heaven, we're all going to worship Jesus, and there won't be any trials to burden us or distract us from our goal. It's only here on earth that we're given the opportunity to praise our Savior during times of sorrow and fear. That's why it's called a sacrifice of praise, I suppose.

"I don't pretend to know what God has in store for my family. There are so many things to worry about. But I know that no matter how bad it gets, once I get to heaven, he'll take that sorrow away. Heal it completely, even if I never find complete comfort here on earth. So what I tell myself when it gets real hard, what I tell myself when I wonder how I can ever possibly thank Jesus for anything when life is so difficult right now — I remind myself that by the time I get to heaven, that sorrow will find perfect healing, and I'll praise my Savior with so much joy and gratitude. And I don't want to be ashamed on that day. I don't want to look back on my life and say, *I wish I'd just trusted God even when things were hard,* or *I wish I'd learned how to praise God during the sorrowful times when I still had the chance.* I take comfort in the reminder that my God never changes, so why should I only praise him when life is going my way?"

Kennedy didn't answer. She was too busy thinking about what happened to Dominic last spring, about the tearful nights that followed, about the dull ache that resurfaced at the most inopportune times.

Sandy let out a little chuckle. "Here I am gabbing away, and I haven't even asked how you're doing. Is everything ok? You hanging in there?"

Kennedy wasn't about to burden Sandy with her own sorrows and uncertainties. Not when Sandy had so many of her own to confront. "I'm all right."

Sandy stole a quick glance at her, enough to show Kennedy she wasn't satisfied with her answer. "Tell me about what's going on in your world. It's been a few weeks since we've had a good sit-down together to talk."

Kennedy tried to think back over the first half of her semester but couldn't even remember what she'd done yesterday morning. "Classes are going well."

Sandy shook her head. "I want to hear about you, sweetheart, not school."

Kennedy should have known from previous experience that she wouldn't get out of this conversation easily.

"And don't be thinking to yourself that I've got too much to worry over to have a good heart-to-heart with you," Sandy added. "Heaven knows I could use some conversation to distract my mind right now."

"In that case," Kennedy began and found herself talking with Sandy about her class schedule, her relationship with Willow, her TA job. She didn't mention the newspaper column she'd written. She didn't even think Sandy realized the editors of the Voice attacked her in last week's article, so she didn't want to bring up how she'd defended her. It all seemed so trivial now compared to what Woong and Carl were suffering.

"And how's your anxiety been?" Sandy asked. "I was

happy when you told me you'd gotten that prescription. Do you think it's helping?"

Kennedy had already wrestled with a lot of guilt for not being able to pray her way out of her PTSD. She doubted Sandy would ever know what a comfort it was for her mentor to affirm her decision like that.

"I think things are getting better," she answered. "I don't worry about having panic attacks out of the blue now. So in that sense I think it really has helped. But then sometimes …" Her voice trailed off, and she wondered how to best express herself.

"Sometimes what, dear?"

Kennedy sighed. "Sometimes I wonder if I took the easy way out. I mean, not with the anxiety and panic so much, but with Dominic. I was really grieving this summer. I think that's when it finally got my parents concerned enough that they made those appointments. And sometimes I feel like …" She didn't know how to finish.

"You feel like taking medicine to take the edge off your grief is dishonoring Dominic's memory?"

Kennedy nodded. "Yeah, something like that. He didn't like the idea of antidepressants or things, at least not in anything but the most extreme cases. And I mean, I know it was pretty bad for me, but I was still functioning all right."

"That's a hard call," Sandy agreed, "but something to bear in mind is that Dominic was never your authority. You're young. You're living on your own now, but in a lot of ways your parents are still the tool God uses to lead you and guide you. The fact that they know you so well that they saw the medicine was at least an option worth exploring says a lot to me. And that you're not having the panic attacks anymore. I know you still grieve for Dominic. Even if the medicine helps you process through that grief more effectively, it doesn't mean you don't feel the pain."

Sandy was right about that. Still, Kennedy hated talking about her own problems. "So how well do you know Dawn's husband?"

Sandy sighed. "Well, Dawn's been working for Carl from the time he came to St. Margaret's. I guess some people are raising a fuss because she only gets paid a part-time stipend — and a very small one at that — even though she does close to full-time work. But that's her choice more than anything else. When we were advertising for the position, it was a paid, hourly wage. She came and interviewed, and once she got the job, she said she didn't need that much money. Her husband works in some kind of financial department. I wouldn't know the details, but he has clients all over the world, takes care of important bank accounts and investments, things like that. I don't know how much he makes, but they have a home out in Newton, so that tells you a lot right there. So once she got the job, Dawn said she didn't need an hourly wage. She'd just take a little stipend to cover gas expenses and stopping for her fancy coffee every morning before work, things like that. The elders were all in agreement that they'd take that extra money just as if they were paying Dawn what any other person would be making, and they'd devote that to missions above the regular budget for giving overseas. It's very generous of Dawn and her husband, really. St. Margaret's has been able to do a lot of good for the kingdom that we otherwise might not have had the resources for."

Kennedy wondered if during her complimentary speech, Sandy had forgotten they were talking about the man accused of kidnapping her son. She replayed the conversation between Sandy and Dawn on the phone. She'd detected a hint of animosity, and she thought Willow had too. Maybe it was because Dawn was married to the man who'd abducted Woong from the hospital. But maybe there was more to it. Dawn had seemed pretty willing to cooperate with the detective. Unless she was sending everybody in the exact opposite direction from where she knew Jackson had taken Woong. But Kennedy had no reason to doubt Dawn's character. She was a little brusque at times, but for a congregation the size of St. Margaret's, a certain level of discretion would definitely be an asset to someone in her position. Still, she didn't meet the stereotype of a chatty church secretary. In fact, Kennedy could see Sandy filling in that role perfectly.

"Did you ever think of doing office work for Carl?" she asked.

Sandy chuckled. "My goodness, no. Carl and I tried that once back at the church plant in New York. It was a disaster."

"Really?"

"Most definitely. After about two hours working together, we realized that it would never do to have one of us bossing the other around. I mean, don't get me wrong, I completely agree with the Bible that a wife should show her husband respect in all things. But the marriage relationship is worlds different than an employee relationship. Carl didn't like giving me orders, and frankly I didn't like taking them. I'm sure there are some marriages where that kind of arrangement would work out just fine, but Carl and me knew it wouldn't work for us. When it comes to the Bible, then absolutely yes, he's the head of our home. But when it comes to our day-to-day lives, we're happy to fuss and fret and come to decisions together. Sometimes he gives in to me, sometimes I give in to him. I know other happy, godly marriages that take a more structural view on the husband's role as head of the wife, but in our marriage, that's never what we've chosen to emphasize."

Kennedy didn't have time to ask any more questions once Sandy pulled into the St. Margaret's parking lot.

"All right. Let's go in and find Dawn."

CHAPTER 32

Kennedy followed Sandy into the foyer. Tables were stacked against all the walls. Boxes of fliers and books were haphazardly strewn about, and there was nobody in sight. Kennedy wondered if all the volunteers had stopped in the middle of their work when they heard what happened to Carl. With his condition being so questionable, would they even hold the conference this weekend?

"Dawn?" Sandy's voice echoed throughout the empty building.

"I'm back here," came the somewhat muffled reply.

Sandy made her way down the hall. Kennedy wondered if maybe they should just wait for Dawn to come to them. Dawn knew what kind of a rush they'd be in, didn't she? Wouldn't she realize how urgent this was?

Sandy stopped outside her husband's office. Kennedy glanced in at Dawn, who was on her knees sweeping up the shattered pieces from the broken bust of Charles Spurgeon. "Such a shame," she muttered without a word of greeting.

"He loved looking at that old fat man with his ridiculous beard."

Sandy helped Dawn up. "I'm so glad you've agreed to come with us and help."

Dawn sniffed. "Least I could do. I don't suppose I need to tell you how truly sorry I am."

"You're not responsible for your husband's actions," Sandy told her. "There's no way you could have known this was what he'd do."

"Well, maybe you're right, but I should have had my eyes open wider. And I shouldn't have been snarky with that detective. It just threw me off guard, you know. I certainly wasn't trying to keep you from your son."

"Of course you weren't. The thought never even crossed my mind." Sandy gave her a hug, which made Dawn bristle.

After their somewhat awkward reconciliation, Dawn brushed her hands off on her pants. "I guess we can clean up the rest of his office once we've got Woong home safe and sound, don't you think?"

"Yes, of course," Sandy replied, and together they all headed out of St. Margaret's and back to Sandy's Honda. Kennedy sat in the back. Sandy and Dawn didn't have much to say to one another other than a few brief directions on where to turn.

"Oh rats," Sandy exclaimed when they were about ten minutes away from the church. "I wanted to pick up another one of Carl's joke books. Now that Woong's learned more of the Bible stories, he can find the humor in a lot of them."

Dawn rolled her eyes. "Your husband must have taken a bad joke class in seminary. He did, didn't he?"

Sandy smiled. "Well, he's been starting his sermons off with a funny story or a riddle or a bad pun for as long as he's been preaching. I'm not sure he picked that up at seminary though."

The women were quiet for a while longer. Kennedy pulled out her phone and checked her email messages. She was surprised to find her inbox so full. A quick browsing of the first few lines explained what it was all about. "Kennedy, I don't know you, but after I read your column in the Voice, I'm glad for that." Or the next one: "As a transgender man, I'm appalled that anyone in this century would think to tell me that my life choices are ordained by the absence or presence of one small piece of anatomy."

Kennedy didn't have the energy for any of this. She'd never asked to become a lightning rod or a target. She skimmed the rest of her inbox. Other than an interview request from some guy who ran a website that focused on issues of censorship and free speech on college campuses, everything else appeared to be an incendiary reaction against her article from yesterday's paper.

She even got an angry message from the parent of one of her lab students. "When Clarisse got a C- on her chemistry midterm, I thought it was because she wasn't studying hard enough. Now that I've seen the sort of drivel her teaching assistant believes, it's no small wonder my child is struggling under your so-called tutelage. I'm actually surprised that your pastor allows you, a young woman, to hold a teaching position at a coed institution."

Kennedy didn't read the rest. Once things calmed down, once Woong was home safe with his mom and Carl was recovered from his injuries, Willow would help her sift through these piles of cyber junk. Her counselor on campus had talked with her several times about her propensity to avoid difficult issues instead of dealing with them straight on, but in this case there was no other option but to ignore the hate.

"We're about forty-five minutes away," Dawn said as she directed Sandy out of the city. Kennedy didn't know where they were going. Couldn't remember if she'd been this way before. She had never been too astute when it came to observing her surroundings, and her sense of direction was almost as deplorable as some of her lab students' sense of entitlement.

"I should call the detective again." Dawn pulled her cell phone out of her designer purse. "Do you think he and his men have made it to the cabin by now?" She glanced at her diamond-studded watch. "I should have paid more attention to the time." She held the phone to her ear and eventually sighed. "No answer. Coverage out that way is spotty at best."

Sandy wasn't very talkative. Kennedy could only imagine what darkness and fear must be swarming around in her spirit. Kennedy had tried so hard to remain hopeful, to imagine that they were simply driving to this cabin to pick up Woong and reunite him with his mother. But what if that's not what happened? What if Dawn's husband panicked? What if he hurt Woong? What if the two of them weren't there at all?

Kennedy's phone beeped with an incoming text. It was from Willow.

Heard anything from Nick? Still haven't been able to reach him. Starting to worry.

Kennedy typed back her response, trying to be as gentle as she could. As much as she cared for her roommate, as happy as she was about her whirlwind, made-in-heaven romance, she didn't have the mental energy to worry about Nick right now. He was an adult and quite capable of taking care of himself.

"I'm still so sorry this happened," Dawn muttered.

Sandy clucked her tongue. "Shh. You don't need to feel guilty at all. Your husband is his own man and responsible for his own actions."

"But I should have known he was planning something." Dawn shook her head and quickly added, "I mean, maybe not something this drastic, but I knew the stress was building up and looking for an outlet."

"So work's been real hard for him lately?" Sandy asked.

"I wish." Dawn laughed mirthlessly. "He was fired, Sandy. He's been out of a job for four months now."

"I'm sorry, dear. I had no idea."

"Yeah, that's the way Jackson wanted it. Wouldn't allow me to tell anybody. Not you, not Carl. It's a big sore spot for him. I thought I was doing the right thing by keeping it quiet like he wanted, but obviously I was wrong."

"How did he lose his job? Did the company downsize?"

"No. I wish to heaven it would have been something that simple. I don't even have all the details, but I can read between the lines well enough. He was forced to resign. Something to do with the way he was handling a client's money. You know I've never been good with numbers and figures. No thanks to Jackson. He never talks to me about work. Doesn't want to worry my pretty little head about it.

Sort of like Carl not coming home and dumping all his church worries on you, I suppose."

Sandy didn't respond, but her lips tightened.

"Anyway," Dawn went on, "at first he just planned to find another line of work. He'd thought about going into consulting before. He was only three years away from getting fully vested in the firm. After that point, he had planned to phase out and start his own business, so at first we figured this was just God's way of speeding up our original plan. But he ran into far more obstacles than he'd expected. He won't come out and say so, but his reputation's basically shot in the finance community. He'd be better off assuming a new name and starting as an hourly bank teller at this point."

"You should have told us, darling. If the two of you have been worried about money …"

"The money's not a problem. Jackson could retire today, and we'd still be set for life, just perhaps without the extra traveling we'd planned on. That's not what's been stressing him out. It's that his whole identity is wrapped up in his job. I thought I had it bad when I became an empty nester, but that was nothing like the identity crisis Jackson's been going through. And I hate to rub on an already sore spot, but this Truth Warriors conference coming up hasn't helped matters either."

"How so?"

"Well, Carl asked Jackson to lead a breakout session. Thought it would be neat for a businessman as successful as my husband to talk about maintaining godly ethics in the workplace. This was planned months before Jackson had to resign, but I know it's been eating him up. And honestly, I can't say that I blame him in this particular instance. I read some of Carl's books from the Truth Warriors movements, or at least I browsed through some of them when things at the office were slow. And if I were a man who'd recently lost his job and felt like his whole life was imploding in around him, I'm not sure how encouraged I'd feel spending the whole weekend being reminded that one of a godly man's primary responsibilities is to provide for his family."

Sandy's jaw was still tense, but there was softness in her voice again. "I'm sure it's been a very difficult time for both of you."

"I had no idea my husband would take it out on Carl like that. I'll testify on oath before every single court in the nation."

"Is it possible we're following the wrong trail?" Sandy wiped a wisp of hair off her forehead and tucked it back into her French braid. "I mean, we've seen the footage of Jackson leaving the hospital with Woong, at least Kennedy and I have. But that doesn't necessarily mean your husband is the one who attacked Carl. You say he was under a lot of stress, that he didn't want to lead a session at the conference this weekend, but that still doesn't explain such a violent …" Sandy didn't finish her thought.

Dawn strummed her manicured fingers against her purse. "I appreciate the good faith you're showing my husband at the moment, but I'm afraid he doesn't deserve it. It wouldn't surprise me in the least to learn that Jackson's responsible for Carl's attack as well as your son's kidnapping."

CHAPTER 33

Kennedy leaned forward slightly in the backseat. She didn't want to miss anything Dawn was going to say.

"Jackson's having a hard time with being between jobs right now. That's only natural. But there's more to it than just that. His issues aren't with Carl specifically, more with conservative Christianity in general, but Carl's the face of that in Jackson's mind. And all this media hype about the Truth Warriors conference has done nothing but rub salt in old wounds.

"Jackson's sister died. It was about ten years ago now, back when we were still living out in Washington. Her husband was no good. She went and talked to her family pastor, and he told her what so many conservative ministers tell their congregants in cases like that. Be more respectful. Be more submissive. Pray for God to change his heart. And unless you've got verifiable proof he's having an affair, you've got no Scriptural basis for divorce.

"Well, she was a devout believer, his sister was. Took

everything that pastor said to heart. Submitted to her husband, prayed for God to change him all the way up to the day he murdered her and their eight-year-old twins with a crowbar."

Kennedy winced and wondered how anyone could get through telling a story like that without the least trace of expression in their voice.

"Jackson was really close to his sister. Had been telling her for years to get out of her marriage. But she was convinced that to leave her husband would be a grave sin, and she took that pastor's advice and sat around waiting for God to change him. Except he never did.

"Like I said, this was years ago, but Jackson's still sore. Still mistrusts any pastor who even hints at wives submitting to their husbands because of what he saw it do to his sister. He'd been handling his grief well for a while, but then the media came and started stirring the pot with their mayhem about the Truth Warriors conference, and I already told you he was feeling insecure about that after losing his job." Dawn shook her head. "I don't want you to think I'm blaming Carl, you know. That man is a treasure of a boss and a joy to work for. But that's the other thing. When these journalists started looking for muck to rake about St. Margaret's, they had a heyday when they found out that the church was paying me so little. They made it out like since I wasn't the one responsible for supporting our family that Carl and the elders chained me to a wall and forced me to take dictation for pennies. Jackson was really scared that it would be one of these sensationalist reporters who found out that he lost his job. You know how these writers can be like sharks. The smallest whiff of blood, a scandal, and they're all right there.

"He wanted me to resign, you know. I fought with him about it. Most of all because I know that if he's sitting around the house moping all day without anything to do, it's only going to make things worse if I'm there bored out of my mind. Jackson kept threatening to go to Carl himself and tell him I was quitting my job. I don't know what Carl would have said about that, but I wonder if that's what happened yesterday afternoon." She shook her head.

Sandy reached over and squeezed her hand. "Whatever his reasons, hon, I don't blame you for them and I don't want you to keep on blaming yourself. Remember Ananias and Saphira in the book of Acts? Each one of them was found guilty before God. Each one had the opportunity to repent independent of each other. God's not looking down at you and holding you accountable for your husband's sins."

Dawn clasped Sandy's hand in hers. "You're an

honorable woman. And I'm sorry for not being a better friend to you. I know it's hard being a pastor's wife, up there on that pedestal you wish nobody would set you up on. I've thought plenty of times you must get lonely up there all by yourself, and every so often I made up my mind to do something about it. Invite you over for some girl time, treat you to a spa day, but I never did. In all honesty, I felt a little intimidated by you. You're like this stay-at-home grandma ninja with the spirit of one of the old-school missionaries and the energy level of a twenty-year-old. And you do it all without pay. Small as my stipend is, I think of myself as a working woman. I put on my business casual, I show up at the office the same time every day, I go home, and at the end of each month I take my little paycheck to the bank and enjoy some spending money. But you, you're raising Woong, you're homeschooling him now on top of all the days you've been watching your grandkids. You oversee the children's ministry and are active in the pregnancy center, and you still manage to make those healthy, delicious home-cooked lunches Carl brings to the office. I guess it's my fault for not taking the time to get to know you better, but part of me assumed that you'd look down at someone like me, a woman who's in the office all day instead of keeping up home or running around town doing good."

Sandy drove with one hand on the steering wheel and one hand still holding Dawn's. "It's such a shame, isn't it, the way we women label each other," Sandy began. "Who's a stay-at-home mom, who's a working woman, who homeschools, who doesn't. The Christian life gives believers so much freedom, but even when we're not judging others for being different than we are, we get the feeling like someone else is judging us. I had no idea what a stigma there was against public school in the homeschool community until I pulled Woong out of Medford Academy. And let me tell you, it's an ugly thing. Whenever a woman's told *you must raise your children exactly this way* or *all wives must behave exactly like this*, you've lost sight of grace. Am I glad I homeschool Woong? Sure am. Turns out it's a great time for us to bond, and I declare I'm learning nearly as much as he is, things I either never studied or have forgotten since I was his age. Does that mean I'll go on homeschooling him until he graduates? Probably not. And it doesn't mean I'm about to vilify every parent who sends their child to public school or private school or makes a choice that's different than mine.

"I think the devil delights in splitting us up. You know, we women have gone through our fair share of trials to get to where we are now. To get to the point where you can work in an office and not have to worry about being harassed on the job. Where I can be involved in the start-up of a new pregnancy center and still not feel like I'm neglecting my duties at home.

"I've met such wonderful moms in the homeschool co-op Woong and I joined. A lot of them are running their own businesses. The mom who's teaching Woong's nutrition class for his science elective, she's got an online coaching business about healthy eating. Another woman, she and her husband write and publish their own homeschool materials. Next spring, they're taking their kids on a nine-month long book tour across the states in their camper. What I'm saying is that there are so many opportunities today that it should be a great time to be a woman. We should celebrate our accomplishments, spur one another on and fan our dreams into flame. Not sit around and bicker like old hens about who buys their kids goldfish crackers from the store and who's cooking gluten-free snacks from scratch. Or who works an outside job and who stays home keeping a picture-perfect house.

"We're so divided, and I think the devil's planned it that way because he knows how important female friendships are, and he's scared of what can happen if we truly do join together in unity and celebrate not only the characteristics that make us women, but the differences that make us unique daughters of our King."

Dawn was quiet for a minute before finally stating, "You should become a motivational speaker or something. I mean it."

Sandy chuckled. "Well, it's kind of you to say so, but I am very content with the role God's given me at this stage of my life. I wouldn't ask for anything more, and I certainly wouldn't ask for anything less."

Kennedy wished Marty and the other editors of the Voice could listen to Sandy. To realize that just because one woman chooses a certain lifestyle it doesn't mean she's making a statement and telling the world it's the only way to live. Why couldn't more people understand that?

They drove for a while without talking, with the soft music from Sandy's hymns playing in the background. When they turned into a wooded area, Kennedy wondered if they were getting closer to the cabin. Just how remote was it?

She tried to channel the fear she was feeling into prayer, but images of Woong alone and scared ran unchecked through her mind. At last, Dawn pointed her finger. "Turn down here. The cabin's about three quarters of a mile away. It's really bumpy, so you want to go slow."

CHAPTER 34

"So do we pull all the way up?" Sandy asked. "Should we call the detective and ask him where to park?"

Dawn shook her head. "You won't get any coverage out here. That's both the blessing and the curse of this place. We used to come out here to relax, get away from the rat race, but the last few years Jackson's been so tied to his phone that he hasn't wanted to unplug for even one night."

Sandy followed a curve in the road and had to stop behind a police car that was blocking the way. She rolled down the window to talk to the officer standing outside.

"I'm Woong's mother. Is my son ok? Have you found him yet?"

Kennedy rolled down her window as well, refusing to miss the officer's words.

The policeman pushed a button and spoke into his radio. "I've got the mother here. Should I send her through?"

Kennedy couldn't make out the reply, but the officer stepped back and told Sandy, "Go on ahead. They're just down the drive about another quarter of a mile."

"What about my son?" Sandy asked with a catch in her voice. "Do they know where my son is?"

The officer's radio hummed to life. "Mom? Is that you?" Woong's voice, though somewhat garbled by static, was unmistakable.

"Oh, thank you, sweet Jesus!" Sandy exclaimed. "Woong? Woong, honey, can you hear me?" She looked up at the officer. "Can he hear me on that thing?"

He smiled. "You want to talk to your son on my radio, or do you want to roll on by and see him for yourself?"

"Myself," Sandy answered breathlessly. "I'll go see him myself, Officer. Thank you so much. Oh, thank you, precious Savior. So he's ok, right?" she asked out her window as she started to roll the Honda forward.

The officer's grin spread wide. "Happy and safe and unharmed. But go see him for yourself. You don't want to take my word for it."

Sandy was laughing while tears streamed down her cheeks. She chuckled away a happy sob. "No, I don't want to take your word for it. Thank you, sir."

Kennedy didn't say anything. Neither did Dawn. Sandy

acted as if she had forgotten there was anyone else in the car with her except for Jesus, and she poured out her profuse praises through her tears.

The Honda slowed to a halt when the cabin came into view, surrounded by at least half a dozen police cars.

"Mom?" The familiar voice carried over the top of Sandy's grateful prayers, and she opened her car door and managed to kneel down in the dirt before Woong ran into her open arms.

"That was wicked awesome!" he shouted. "Mr. Jackson told me he had a present for Dad, and I needed to come with him to the parking lot to help him carry it up, only when we got to the car, he said he musta left it at his house. So we started driving, and I've already talked with the police officer, Mom, so I know I didn't do the right thing just then, but he was an adult and wasn't a stranger, so I thought I had to obey him. So I hope you'll forgive me that part, because I really wasn't trying to be naughty or stuff and nonsense like that. But then we started driving, and we kept driving and driving and driving, and I could tell by the signs we weren't in Cambridge no more, and from the looks of all the trees in the woods it was like we weren't anywhere no more, so I asked Mr. Jackson about it, and he said that the present was a real bearskin rug that he shot on this island way up in

Alaska. And I never seen a rug like that, so I got real curious, and then he took me to this cabin and it wasn't just the rug, but there was a whole stuffed deer. I'm not talking about the kind of baby toy you get in the store, neither, but a real live deer, except it weren't alive no more on account of Mr. Jackson shooting it. Right in the head, too, and you can see the part between its eyes where the taxi man — that's the one who stuffed the deer to begin with — had to use some fake hair on account of not wanting there to be a bullet hole right there on his face. So anyway, I knew enough by then to figure you'd be pretty worried about me, only Mr. Jackson said that cell phones don't work all the way out here, but that he'd left you a message so you'd come and meet us, and then we'd all go camping. Well, it sounded a little fishy to me on account of you liking the kinds of vacations with nice houses that serve you big fancy breakfasts in the morning, only you never said anything before about enjoying camping, and even though Mr. Jackson said that we could go hunting, I couldn't picture you holding one of them big guns and blowing the brains out of a cute little deer or stuff and nonsense like that.

"So that's when I figured I'd been kidnapped, only I couldn't let Mr. Jackson know that I'd caught on, so I just had to go along with it. I had it all planned out, too. I was gonna wait until he was asleep, and then I found some fishing poles and whatnot in this little shed, kinda like a garage only there were no cars parked in there on account of it being too little, but it was messy like a garage, and there were these fishing poles, so what I decided I'd do was wait until Mr. Jackson was asleep, and then I'd come get the string and tie him up real good with it. Because that time Dad took me fishing, I remember how the string looks real thin, only it's strong enough to cut your finger, so I figured that since I couldn't find no rope, it would do to tie up Mr. Jackson and then escape. Except that's not what happened. Turns out I didn't have to tie anybody up after all. Mr. Jackson said I could pick out a movie, so I chose one of the Pixar ones. He had the Avengers, too, and I hafta admit I got a little tempted to watch that even though I know you think it's too violent for me. But I figured that once I escaped you'd want me to tell you exactly what happened, and I didn't wanna make you sad, so I chose one of the Toy Story movies I hadn't seen yet, and it was pretty good, only I didn't get to finish it because I was sitting there watching, and Mr. Jackson, he was working at this desk in the kitchen doing something on his computer way over in the other room, and all of a sudden there was a loud *pow*! And the door just broke right in two, and the next thing I knew this big old policeman had picked me up and carried me outside, and they told me I was safe, and that you were coming to get me. Which is exactly what happened."

Sandy had started crying about halfway into Woong's story, but he was so engrossed in the retelling that he didn't notice until he was done. "Aww, Mom," he whined and submitted himself to his mother's tearful hugs and smothering kisses for a few seconds before wiggling himself free.

Peering into the backseat, Woong gave a giant smile. "Hi, Kennedy. Did Willow and Nick come, too? I can't wait to tell Willow that I met a bear all the way from Alaska. Do you think maybe she saw that very same bear one day before Mr. Jackson shot it?"

Kennedy was too relieved to find Woong talkative and unharmed to worry about something like a geography lesson about how big the state of Alaska really is. "You'll have to ask her when you see her."

"Yeah, I'm ready to go back to Cambridge now. I'm awfully hungry. I told Mr. Jackson it was past my lunch time, but all he did was heat up one little can of ratiolis or whatever that kind of pasta it is with the cheese on the inside and covered in spaghetti sauce."

Sandy gave him one more hug as Detective Drisklay

walked up. For the first time that Kennedy could remember, both his hands were empty.

"Doesn't look like he's been hurt at all," he declared flatly.

"Thank you, Jesus," Sandy breathed.

Drisklay frowned. "Well, we got Jackson. Not that he put up much of a fight. He's on his way to the police department now, but I thought you might want to know that in addition to kidnapping your son, he also confessed to attacking your husband. Something about wanting his wife to quit her job at the church only she wouldn't listen. Of course, nothing is admissible yet, and his lawyer may try to get him to rescind his original statement, so I can't tell you the case is closed, but unofficially, I thought it might put your mind at ease to know that we got the right man."

"I appreciate that, detective," Sandy replied. "Words can't tell you how relieved I am to have my son back safe and sound." She glanced at Dawn who was still in the passenger seat. "Can you let us know what's going to happen now to Jackson?"

Drisklay peered into the window and frowned at Dawn. "You the wife?" he asked flatly.

Dawn nodded her head, her expression as stoic as the detective's.

"I got a message for you from your husband." Drisklay coughed. His voice was hoarse. "Since he cooperated with us during the arrest, and since you're the one who led us here, I told him I'd pass his words on to you. If you want to hear them, that is."

Dawn sat up a little taller in her seat. "I'm ready whenever you are."

Drisklay gave her a small tilt of the head. If Kennedy didn't know the detective better, it would have looked like a nod of respect.

"Your husband wanted me to tell you that he's very, very sorry."

CHAPTER 35

The drive back to Cambridge was partly like an impromptu worship session, with Sandy regularly breaking out into prayer or song, and partly like a children's slumber party, with Woong talking so fast he was the equivalent of four or five different kids rolled into one. Kennedy was glad he was unharmed. She didn't know if under the surface he'd been more scared than he cared to publicly admit, but right now he seemed to relish the extra attention, and each time he told the story of his capture and rescue it grew more and more embellished. She wouldn't be surprised if by tomorrow Woong was telling everyone that he fought Jackson off with his bare hands.

Dawn was quiet, and Kennedy was conscious of the awkward situation she and Sandy found themselves in, but she didn't know how to ease any of that tension. Her phone beeped almost immediately after they got back on the main highway headed back to Cambridge. She'd missed a call. Praying it wasn't another hate message, she listened to her voicemail.

"This is Devorah Adell attempting to reach Kennedy Stern. Kennedy, I have to confess that I'm disappointed in you. When Dr. Faber threatened to fire you from my lab, I told him you were a model student, the epitome of responsibility and respectability. I hate to inform you that there's nothing respectable about missing a meeting your professor and perhaps your most vocal advocate has gone through the efforts of setting up for you. Seeing as how it's already ten minutes to four, I have no choice but to leave your future as a TA in my class up to Dr. Faber's judgment. If you'd like to try to reach him before his office hours end at 5:30, you're more than welcome to try. Good day."

Kennedy looked at the time. How could she have forgotten?

"What is it, dear?" Sandy asked, glancing at Kennedy in the rearview mirror.

"I missed a meeting this afternoon. A pretty important one." How could she be so stupid? How hard would it have been to call and cancel before driving with Sandy all around Massachusetts? Her professor was right. Adell might be her only supporter right now. How could she have forgotten something so serious?

"Could you reschedule?" Sandy asked.

Kennedy did the math. If Sandy dropped her off at the T

station, she could probably make it back to campus to meet Dr. Faber in his office. The bigger question was did she really want to? Why should she keep on working in a department that was so quick to profile her after reading one single article she wrote? But if she didn't show up, if she didn't humble herself before Faber and beg to get her job back, wouldn't that reflect poorly on Adell who'd stood up for her?

No, she had to make that appointment, or at least she had to try.

"I know you want to get back to be with Carl as soon as possible," Kennedy said, "but do you think you could drop me off by the Red Line?"

"I'll take you back to campus myself, sweetie. It's only a few minutes out of the way. I don't mind."

"No, I want you to be with Carl. I know it's been hard for you being gone from him for so long. I think if you take me to the T station, I'll still be able to meet with the professor before he goes home for the day."

"If you're sure, honey."

Kennedy nodded. "I'm sure."

"What's the meeting about?"

She shut her eyes, trying to escape from the guilt and stress that pounded down on her. "Just about the lab I teach. Nothing all that interesting."

CHAPTER 36

"So you're the infamous Kennedy Stern." Dr. Faber leaned back in his chair and studied her over the top of his glasses. "Have we met before?"

"You were on the panel when I interviewed for the med school early acceptance program."

Faber nodded. "I see. Did I let you in?"

She nodded.

He cleared his throat. "Well, since you're here, may as well ask you to sit down."

"I'm really sorry I missed our appointment earlier," she began.

He shrugged. "No need to apologize to me. It's Dr. Adell who scheduled that meeting to begin with."

"Well, it was wrong for me to miss it. I feel terrible. We had something of an emergency with some friends …"

"Your pastor?" he interrupted.

She stared.

"He's been on the news. I'm not so calloused that I don't

care if someone's been attacked and left in a coma."

Kennedy didn't reply.

Faber stared at her. She couldn't tell if his expression was his version of a smile or a scowl. "So, tell me what I can do for you today."

Kennedy wasn't prepared for his question. She'd been expecting a lecture.

"I'd like to keep working as a TA," she stammered.

Faber leaned back in his chair. "Yes, Adell tells me you're quite gifted for an undergrad student."

Kennedy couldn't figure out if he was being condescending or not. Mustering up her sense of confidence, she continued, "I know my article got some people upset, but first of all, my opinion on things like politics or religion really has nothing to do with how well I can teach a lab class. Second of all, I think a lot of people are misinterpreting what I wrote in the first place. I never said that all women should stay at home and take care of the kids. I just said that we should have more respect for those who do."

Faber's expression didn't change. "So tell me, Miss Stern, what were your thoughts when you were admitted into the early acceptance program at Harvard?"

Kennedy didn't know what an application that she sent in nearly four years ago had to do with her article on women's rights and roles, but she didn't want to antagonize Dr. Faber, especially since he'd been on the committee that accepted her into the prestigious program. "I was very honored. I don't think words can express how excited I was."

"And is that because in the household and religious structure in which you were raised, women weren't expected to receive higher educational opportunities?"

Kennedy blinked. "No. It was because I worked really hard in high school so that I could one day become a doctor."

"And was it concerning to you or to your family that you might start out your time in college, fall in love, and get married? What if you have kids? Do you just plan to tell the admissions committee of Harvard Medical School that everything they invested in your education was for nothing because you're going to drop out and become a stay-at-home mom?"

Kennedy wondered if Dr. Faber, brilliant as he must be to head the science department at Harvard University, had even read her article. "I thought this discussion was about whether or not I could continue teaching in the lab."

"All right then." Faber interlaced his fingers and set them in front of him on his desk. "Let's talk about your lab. I received two phone calls today from parents very distraught that their children are being subjected to misogynistic biases."

Misogynistic biases? "Just what do you think I'm teaching these students?"

"I'm sure I don't know," Faber replied, "which is why it would have been convenient if you had kept our original appointment with Adell, who apparently is ready to stick her academic reputation on the line for someone who doesn't even have the decency to reschedule a meeting that her professor has worked quite hard to set up."

Kennedy was about to mention Woong's kidnapping, but Faber went on without pause.

"Furthermore, as a student who's been invited into the early admissions medical program at our school, you represent our science department specifically and Harvard University in general whether you feel up to the task or not. And frankly, your column defending dangerous and oppressive patriarchal ideology is simply not the image that we want associated with Harvard University, its science department, or its medical school."

"What are you saying exactly?" Kennedy asked and braced herself for Faber's answer.

"I'm saying that unless I see a printed retraction of your views in the Voice, I not only will have to terminate your privileges as a teaching assistant in the science department, I'll have to take a long and serious look at your provisional admittance to the medical school, an admittance I'd like to remind you that is contingent on your keeping up your grades and your conduct in a manner befitting a student at our university."

CHAPTER 37

Twenty minutes later Kennedy had returned to her dorm room and told her roommate everything about Woong's rescue and her meeting with the head of the science department.

"Dude," Willow exclaimed after Kennedy mentioned Dr. Faber's ultimatum. "So what are you going to do?"

"I still haven't decided yet. I'm going to call my dad this evening. It's too early now. Besides, it's been such a stressful two days anyway that I didn't want to make any rash decisions."

"I would have told that hoity-toity professor exactly where to take his threats, and I would have walked right out of there."

"I guess maybe if it was just getting fired as a TA. But this isn't just a four-hour-a-week job we're talking about anymore. This is my whole career."

Willow applied some of her eye shadow. "Dude," she repeated.

"What about you?" Kennedy asked. "Are you doing ok? Have you heard from Nick yet?"

"Yeah, I got a quick text. Said he was going out for a drive and not to worry. He does that every once in a while. Turns off his phone and just takes off. I think it helps him unwind. I know the situation with Carl has gotten him really upset. I shouldn't worry about him so much, but I can't help it."

"That's because you love him."

Willow focused on filing her nail. "I really do. It's funny. I've had more boyfriends than I'd ever want to try to count, so you'd think I might have already been jaded by love or whatnot. But I've never experienced anything like what I have with Nick before. I used to think about marriage, about how unnatural it was to choose one mate and stick with them for the rest of your life. I used to think it was the epitome of hubris to assume that you knew yourself well enough, let alone your partner, to be able to decide if you should commit to a lifetime together. But with Nick …" Willow paused to study herself in the mirror.

"Anyway, I just hope you find the same thing one day. I know you and Dominic were taking things slow, and who knows what might have happened if you'd had more time together, but believe it or not, it's actually something I started praying about for you."

Kennedy couldn't help laughing. "You're praying that God will send me someone to marry?"

Willow looked hurt. "I'm being serious now. I sometimes feel bad because Nick and I have this really special thing going on. I know you're still getting over what happened with Dominic. But what I'd love more than anything is if God were to send somebody your way so we could share our special relationships together. Sandy told me something a few weeks ago, and I've been thinking about it a lot. I was telling her it's wicked hard to think of staying totally abstinent until Nick and I get married, and I joked and said something like we should just go elope one weekend and get it over with. But she told me not to rush these days. Said that as much as she loves Carl and as close as they've grown over the years, there was something really special about the time they were together right before he proposed and then before they got married. You think I'm a big dork, don't you?"

"No, of course I don't."

"Yes, you do. I can see it in your eyes. Well, you just remember. One day, you and I are going to be little old ladies, twice as old as Sandy, and we'll be sitting in rocking chairs knitting little booties for our great-grandbabies and reminiscing about the good old days, and you'll say, *remember when I was so sad because I missed my old boyfriend so much? And we had that talk about you and Nick and how no matter how close you grow to your spouse over the years, there's nothing quite like those months leading up to the wedding, hard as they may be and impatient as your horny little body might get? You remember that? Well, Willow, you were absolutely right. And Mr. Wonderful and I, we've had the most incredible marriage anyone could imagine, visiting no less than two hundred different countries on our medical mission trips and raising those ten delightful kids of ours and welcoming our ninety delightful grandbabies into the world, but there's nothing like falling in love for the very first time. You were absolutely right about that.*"

Kennedy finally gave in to a chuckle.

"There's a smile," Willow exclaimed, and then her face grew serious. "If it's too soon for you to be thinking this way, just tell me. I'm not trying to make things harder on you."

"I know that."

"So we're ok?" Willow asked hopefully.

"Yeah, we're ok."

Willow grinned and jumped over to slide in next to Kennedy on her bed. "Good. Because I've been dying to ask about your breakfast this morning."

Kennedy couldn't remember what she had to eat. "What breakfast?"

Willow rolled her eyes, revealing glittery purple eyeshadow. "Your breakfast," she repeated with significance. "With Ginger?"

"You mean Ian?"

Willow shrugged. "Ginger, Ian, what's the difference when he's that hot?" She scooted closer. "So, how'd it go? Did you have a good time? What did you talk about? Did he interview you for a story? Will it be in the paper? You haven't told me anything."

Kennedy sank back against her pillow. "It was just breakfast."

"Sure it was." Willow pulled Kennedy's pillow out from behind her and swatted her playfully with it. "Come on. There's got to be more to it than that. Did you enjoy yourself? Did you run out of things to talk about? Did he pay? Did you go Dutch? Tell me something. This has been like the longest day of my entire life. The least you can do is get my mind off all my worries and spare at least one or two juicy details."

"No juicy details." Kennedy was glad the pillow was still covering half her face so Willow couldn't catch her trying to hide her grin.

"What do you mean no juicy details? You were out for almost two hours before I had to track you down. Don't tell me you spent that whole time on the interview and nothing else."

Kennedy grabbed the pillow when her roommate tried to lift it off her face. "No juicy details," she protested again, but her voice betrayed her by a laugh.

Willow smacked her once more. "I knew it. So come on. Tell me. What all did you talk about? Do you like him? Is he a Christian? Are you going to see him again?"

Kennedy stopped giggling when her cell rang. Willow reached over and picked it up from the desk. "It's Sandy calling." She handed the phone to Kennedy.

"Hello?" She tried to make her voice sound serious, worrying it might hurt Sandy's feelings to know she had found anything to laugh about on a day like this.

Sandy sounded flushed. "Kennedy?" That one single word made Kennedy's heart swell with hope.

"Yeah?" Her own tone matched Sandy's excited one. Even Willow must have picked up on the change because she leaned forward, trying to get her ear as close to Kennedy's phone as possible.

"Glorious news, dear. Carl still hasn't woken up, but the brain swelling went down so dramatically after the prayer meeting that they decided to test him one more time without the ventilator. He's doing just fine. If we keep seeing this kind of steady progress, they'll take him off the machine this evening."

CHAPTER 38

Kennedy had never seen Willow drive as fast as she did that night on the way to Providence Hospital. She thought about an old adage her mom used to say: *Trials and blessings always come in threes.* With Carl on the ventilator, Woong kidnapped, and Kennedy about to lose her job as a TA, the first half of the proverb had certainly appeared true. Kennedy was grateful to receive some good news for a change.

They got stuck in rush hour traffic and got to Carl's room in the ICU right after they took out his breathing tube. Technically, visiting rights were reserved for immediate family members only, but Sandy talked the sympathetic nurse into letting Kennedy and Willow come in if they promised not to stay long.

Woong was in a corner with one of his dad's Bible joke books, occasionally breaking out into a smile and looking no worse off after being kidnapped and rescued. Sandy was flushed. Nearly half her hair had fallen out of her braid, but there was a radiance that shined around her and filled the room with so much joy Kennedy couldn't have felt sad even if she wanted to.

"The Lord is so good. The Lord is so good," Sandy repeated over and over as she related to the girls what had happened that afternoon.

When they first got back to Providence after saving Woong, Carl's condition was basically unchanged. "And I wasn't too disappointed," Sandy remarked. "If he had gotten a lot better or a lot worse while I wasn't here to look after him, I would have felt terribly guilty."

Drisklay had questions for Woong, so he and Sandy met with the detective in the ICU conference room. Dawn waited in the lobby for the detective to take her to the police department so she could speak with her husband.

Sandy clucked her tongue. "I know the poor woman feels awful about what happened. I just pray that Jesus shows her his truth so she doesn't keep beating herself up for her husband's crimes."

After Drisklay left, Sandy and Woong went back to Carl's bedside. "It was Woong who noticed the change first. Something different about Carl's face. He wasn't so pale, and he stopped looking like he was in a coma and more like he was just in a deep sleep. I didn't want to call the nurse in right away. I didn't want to find out it was just wishful thinking or something like that. But when she came in to check his vitals, she noticed it, too, and said his numbers were the best they'd been all day. The doctor asked me if I wanted to turn off the machine just for a short time. Nothing dangerous at all. It would just tell them if Carl could breathe on his own or not. Well, I felt so encouraged by how much stronger he looked, so I said, 'Ok, let's do it.'

"I was so scared I was shaking because the whole time I'd been talking with the doctors there was this little voice in the back my head that told me I was making it all up. There weren't any improvements, and there wouldn't be any improvements. But then they turned the machine off, and we all waited, and Carl just kept on breathing peacefully like he was taking one of his Sunday afternoon naps. Well, he was still working a little harder than he should have to keep his numbers up, so the doctor wanted to keep the machine running as backup, but then they tried it again this evening, and praise the Lord, he's holding perfectly steady."

"That's great news." Willow gave Sandy a hug and then let out a surprised, "Oh," as if she'd been startled. Kennedy turned to see Nick in the doorway with his head hung low, his dreads trailing behind him like the tail of a lost little puppy.

CHAPTER 39

"Nick!" Willow ran toward him but stopped halfway to the door. "What is it? What's wrong?"

Nick's face was pale. He appeared almost clammy. Willow took him by the arm and sat him down on the doctor's swivel chair.

"You know," she began, "I should be wicked mad at you for deserting me like you did today, except you look like you got hit by a truck. What happened?" Her voice was full of tenderness.

Nick shook his head. His dreadlocks, usually so animated, hung limp past his shoulders. "I'm a terrible, horrible person."

Willow stood behind him, rubbing his back. "Don't talk like that. You had a bad day, that's all. So tell me what the matter is. I'm done lecturing you. Now I just want to help you feel better."

"There are some things I've got to get off my chest first." Nick turned to Sandy and took both her hands in his. "Sandy, I am so sorry for taking advantage of you and Carl's friendship for so long. We'd gotten so close, close as family, and like family, I began to grow resentful." He sniffed. "I should have never treated your husband the way I did. All those fights, the accusations. I think what got me so worked up — aside from seeing Carl on the ventilator which is bad enough — was realizing that I'm no better than whatever thug did this to him. I've got just as many anger issues, just as much hatred in my heart. So I came here to apologize."

He let go of Sandy's hands. Clutching the side of the bed, he lowered himself to his knees and rested his forehead near Carl's pillow.

"Pastor Carl," he began in a shaky voice. "Friend. Brother. You've been more of a father to me than anyone else in the past decade. And like the prodigal son, I've made a fool of myself. Let our disagreements get in the way of our friendship. I hate to confess it, but I have to. Over the last several months in particular, I've allowed so much hardness and resentment to creep into my heart. Tarnish my opinion of you. I haven't shown you the respect you deserve as my pastor, my employer, and my mentor.

"We've always had our disagreements, but things got really bad when you began planning that Truth Warriors conference. And there are still a lot of things about it that I don't agree with, but that certainly doesn't mean that you're the misogynistic monster the media has made you out to be.

You love and honor your wife in a way that is truly selfless. I can only hope to be half the man you are one day. You speak out openly against how degrading and demeaning pornography is to women, and I know God has used you and that little blue book of yours to lead dozens of men out of their addictions. The more I wanted to side with the media against you, the more I realized that even though we might have different views on exactly how to love our brothers and sisters in Christ, nobody with two eyes in their head could accuse you of being anything but the epitome of sacrificial, godly love. The more I thought about it, the more I realized how far I have to go in my own walk with Christ before I can learn to love and serve as selflessly as you do.

"When I found you knocked out in your office, I was so scared. Scared of losing you. Scared that I would never be able to tell you how sorry I am that I've allowed this wall of resentment to grow up between us. You more than anyone else have taught me that it's possible for two believers to share their deep fellowship even when they disagree. Forgive me, brother. Forgive me for forgetting that when you found me and took me in, I was so broken and beat up by the world, floundering in my faith and about to give up all hope in the Lord. But you picked me up. Dragged me up is more like it, out of that mud and showed me the solid rock

I could stand on. If it hadn't been for you, I probably would have given up on God years ago. But you didn't let that happen. And I never thanked you for that, and now I'm so scared that you won't ever wake up. That I'll never get the chance to tell you how much I love you."

By the time Nick was finished talking, Carl and Woong were the only two in the room with dry eyes. Kennedy, sensing how inappropriate it was for her to be here witnessing a scene so intimate, focused on Woong, who smiled to himself as he turned the pages in his father's joke book.

"That was beautiful," Sandy breathed and tried to help Nick back up on his feet.

"Not so fast," he said. Still on his knees, he reached out to Willow and made her stand in front of him.

"What are you doing?" she whispered.

"Oh, just about the most terrifying thing I've ever done in my life, that's all." He let out a nervous chuckle. "Willow Winters, for years I've been asking God to send me a partner. Someone who shares my love for the Lord, my desire to see justice reign on the earth, my passion for ministry. On the day I met you, I knew that you were the one that God had planned for me to meet, fall passionately in love with, and spend the rest of my life with."

Willow tried to pull him off the ground, but Nick took hold of both her hands again and made her face him. "At the risk of sounding ridiculously mushy, I have never met anyone who's made me feel so excited about life. So eager to serve the Lord. So expectant about the future God has planned for us. Last summer, I asked you to pray and seek God's heart to discern if this romance was truly destined to blossom into something permanent. I've been praying, too, and I know beyond any doubt that if you stand here in agreement with me, nothing would bring me more joy than to spend the rest my life worshiping and serving God side by side with you as my partner, my soulmate, and my spouse."

He searched several of his pants pockets before he pulled out a small box. "I know it was a bad day to leave you alone, and I'm sorry for that, but I needed to think and make sure that now was the right time. I also needed to look for this." He opened the box and stared up at Willow with joyful, shining eyes. "Willow Winters, will you marry me?"

"Yes, you silly thing, now get off the floor before you hurt your knees." Willow lifted him to his feet once he slipped on the ring. "This is beautiful. Where did you find it?"

"I knew how you felt about blood diamonds, so I went to the free trade store to see what kind of jewelry they had there.

This particular ring was made by girls and women living in a safe house in Vietnam who have been rescued from a life of sex slavery. I chose it as a symbol of the way I believe God will use our union and our ministry together to stand up for the rights of the oppressed and to make the world a more just, beautiful, glorious place."

Willow showed off the beaded ring to Kennedy and then to Sandy who sat in a corner dabbing her eyes with a tissue.

"I am so happy for you two," she exclaimed.

"Yes, of course, we're all happy." Carl's voice from the hospital bed made everyone turn.

Sandy gasped and rushed to her husband's side.

He smiled faintly and tried to raise himself from his pillow. "Now, Nick, don't you think it's about time to kiss your fiancée?"

CHAPTER 40

Kennedy couldn't remember a twenty-four-hour period filled with so much of both heartache and joy. By the time she and Willow returned back to campus, she was exhausted.

"What a day," Willow sighed.

Kennedy's thoughts exactly.

They were quiet on the walk to their dorm. They'd stayed far past the typical ICU visiting hours, but Carl had shown so much improvement once he woke up that the nurse didn't have the heart to send anyone away.

Kennedy still couldn't believe her roommate was engaged. She figured Nick would end up proposing one day, but she'd been sure they'd wait until Willow was at least a senior to make things official. Kennedy didn't have the heart to ask Willow how soon they'd plan the wedding. Would she need to find herself a new roommate before graduation?

Carl had surprised them all when he woke up from his coma in the middle of Nick's proposal. It took several minutes before Nick mustered the courage to ask if he'd been awake during his apology and confession as well. Carl said he slept right through it but asked Nick to give a repeat (albeit abridged) performance.

Woong had been so excited when his dad woke up. He wanted to tell Carl all about getting kidnapped and rescued, but his mom shushed him and told him she'd tell him about it a little later once he had a chance to recover some of his strength. So instead, Woong asked if Carl heard any of the jokes from the book he'd been reading to him.

"Jokes?" Carl frowned. "Well, let me think. I don't remember hearing any jokes, but I've got a new one for you. Do you know why there are no potholes on the way to heaven?"

After asking what a pothole was, Woong said he was stumped.

His dad smiled. "Because Jesus paved it all."

Any concerns about Carl's long-term recovery were put to rest in that one evening. The doctors would still monitor him in the hospital, but it was clear to everyone that they bore witness to some sort of miracle, whether medical or divine or both.

Kennedy's heart was full in spite of how exhausted she felt. It was past nine when they walked up to their dorm. The graffiti on the wall had already been painted over.

"Well, look who that is."

Kennedy turned at the familiar voice. Ian was sitting on a bench beneath a security light, an open book on his lap. "I was wondering if I'd catch you tonight."

Willow made a dramatic show of digging through her purse. "Oh, I completely forgot, I need to call Nick and talk to him about that thing we were supposed to talk about tonight when I called. Sorry to be rude and run off, but I don't want to keep him waiting." She scurried into the dorm, leaving Kennedy outside with Ian.

He smiled. "Hey."

"Hey."

"Long day?"

"You could say that."

Ian stood up and stretched. "Care to take a walk and tell me about it?"

Kennedy thought about her nine o'clock class the next morning. About the decision she'd have to make to write that redaction and keep her guaranteed admission to medical school or not. About all the talking and giggling and wedding planning Willow would be sure to want her to join in over the next months.

She found it easy to return Ian's smile. "Sure."

Forty-five minutes later, seated in front of his empty plate at L'Aroma Bakery, Ian let out a sigh. "So have you decided what you're going to do about the medical school thing?"

"I don't know. I want to talk it over with my dad before I make any big decisions." Why did she say that? Was she twelve years old all over again?

There was something in Ian's eyes, but she couldn't tell what it was. Amusement? Respect? "Well, if you want to make a big fuss about it, let me know. I've got a few friends very interested in cases of free speech on college campuses."

"Thanks. I've already gotten a few emails from people like that."

"Just be careful who you talk to. You're welcome to run the names by me, and I can tell you who's legit and who's just looking for a pretty face for their clickbait articles."

Kennedy was glad the lights at L'Aroma were dim so he couldn't see her blush. Maybe it was just because of Willow's good news and Carl's miraculous recovery, but she didn't think she'd enjoyed herself so much in one evening before.

Ian closed the little book he'd used to jot down a few notes while they talked about Kennedy's article in the Voice and about the drama the Lindgrens had lived through that day. He was such a good listener Kennedy couldn't even tell what his own opinions were on certain matters, but he knew how to ask the right kinds of questions that helped her process the thoughts and half-conceived ideas that had been swirling around in her brain.

Ian looked at the time. "Well, it's getting late. You probably have class tomorrow, don't you?"

"First thing in the morning," Kennedy answered.

"Can I walk you back to campus?"

"Sure." She heard Willow's voice in the back of her head. *First dates are so romantic.* She couldn't turn the recording off, not that she was sure she wanted to.

She gave Ian a smile and let him hold the door open for her as they walked out of L'Aroma Bakery into the clear night. Stars twinkled overhead, stars that whispered to Kennedy promises of hope and joys to come.

ACKNOWLEDGEMENTS

Abridged deals with two topics I feel very strongly about: free speech and women's rights. As an author and a book lover, I stand against censorship. Like O'Brien, the editor Kennedy works with on Harvard's student newspaper, I would much rather read books by people who believe differently than I do and be challenged by their viewpoints than restrict myself to authors who share my exact same opinions.

Unfortunately, college campuses are notorious for limiting the free speech of their students in the name of tolerance. It might sound far-fetched, but students have been censored for "crimes" even less threatening than Kennedy's column in the paper.

The question of a woman's role in the church and society is quite touchy, which is why it was a topic I wanted to highlight and address in *Abridged.* I especially stand by Sandy's comments when she's in the car with Dawn, that women should never pit themselves against one another based on differences in lifestyles. Additionally, no matter what your stance is on the role of women in the church, I think we can all use a reminder to be praying for girls and women in other cultures who are barred from the most basic educational and vocational opportunities because of their gender.

One of my favorite parts about the more recent Kennedy books is watching Woong grow and mature. If you didn't know already, Woong has his own novel that tells about his life in Korea before his adoption. His book is called *Flower Swallow*, which has won both an Illumination Book Award and a Moonbeam Book Award.

I'm so thankful for my prayer team for praying another novel into existence, and I'd like to publicly thank God for giving me the physical and emotional strength to put out another book.

My husband is so supportive, and as a pastor and something of a politics junkie, he has really helped me flesh out some of my own convictions regarding both free speech and women's rights.

A big thanks to my friend Tamara for fielding some medical questions and to my editors for catching so many of my messy mistakes.

I hope you enjoyed this novel, and I look forward to sharing Kennedy's next adventure with you soon!

DISCUSSION QUESTIONS

For group discussion or personal reflection

I hope you enjoyed *Abridged*. If you'd like to chat about the novel with a book club (or you just want some time for personal reflection), here are some questions to get you going.

Issue-Based Questions

1. Have you ever read a book that changed your mind about a particular topic?
2. Do you appreciate reading books or articles by authors who believe differently than you?
3. Were there any books you weren't allowed to read as a child? What about TV shows or movies?
4. What is your church's stance on a woman's role in the church? Do you agree or disagree with it?

5. Have you ever felt marginalized at church because of your gender?
6. How do you feel about conferences like the fictional Truth Warriors events mentioned in this story?
7. Do you consider yourself a feminist? What does that word mean to you?

Story-Related Questions

1. Do you think what Kennedy experienced after writing her article in the school paper is realistic?
2. Have you heard of other cases of academic censorship like this occurring on college campuses?
3. Do you think Kennedy should retract her article?
4. How have you felt about Willow's growth as a character and the recent developments in her life?
5. Which part of the plot surprised you the most?
6. Do you have any close friendships with someone who strongly disagrees with you?
7. Have you ever lost a friendship because of different political or theological views?

Books by Alana Terry

Kennedy Stern Christian Suspense Series

Unplanned

Paralyzed

Policed

Straightened

Turbulence

Infected

Abridged

Whispers of Refuge (Christian suspense set in North Korea)

The Beloved Daughter

Slave Again

Torn Asunder

Flower Swallow

See a full list at www.alanaterry.com

Made in the USA
Middletown, DE
24 June 2020